To my awesome Auntie,
thank you for years of
enthusiastic support.
I love you.

Opus Aria

By LL Lemke

To everyone who has supported me while

chasing this dream down.

CHAPTER 1

Aria Brayton stared at the holoboard in front of her with fear. There was a picture of her and her brightly dyed pink hair staring back at her blankly. The bold font spelled out 'wanted for the murder of several international emissaries'. It showed exactly what she was – an enhanced human, a person with an artificial intelligence unit. Dangerous and different. This had Project Maestro written all over it and the mere thought of them getting their hands on her and her AI, Piano, made her skin crawl. She toyed with removing her 'wanted poster' from the rotation of images, but she knew it would be traced and they would know where she and Piano were. She couldn't risk that.

"Piano, please scan for AIs. Now," Aria whispered into her mind.

"Right away, Aria."

She stared at the image for a few more moments, it was an older picture; she was fourteen or fifteen. While she was currently twenty-three, her face wasn't too different than the picture. She sighed in frustration; her hair was currently the same vibrant pink that the image displayed. While she changed her appearance every few weeks, Aria had a tendency to dye her hair back to pink. It felt more normal than her natural dirty blonde hair. She ran her fingers through the hologram, making it disappear for a second, her blank blue-green eyes splitting into five and then reuniting. Horror broke through her mind and sat, heavy, in the pit of her stomach and tightened the muscles in the back of her neck. Project Maestro was after them again.

Aria glanced around the nearly deserted cafe, hoping that no one had seen the hologram. The people in the place looked defeated, their heads leaning on the table next to the obligatory cup of coffee. The waitress was nowhere to be seen. It wasn't like the hologram was big – it was maybe the size of the dinner plates that were littered on some of the tables. No, no one in the café was paying attention to the holoboard rotation.

She walked calmly back to her booth and waited as patiently as she could for the food that she had ordered. Piano had been with Aria for ten years. Project Maestro had paired them together carefully. A person could feasibly be paired with multiple AIs, but Project Maestro had erred on the side of caution and researched their AIs and paired them with a subject that had a similar personality. They also leaned towards caution because removing an AI was deadly, mainly due to the implantation location.

"I don't feel any AIs in this area. Eat and get out of this place quickly, let's not draw unneeded attention to ourselves."

Ever since they had come back to this universe from Night City, they had been running. She had sometimes done work with her friend Babylon – the man with metal fingers and toes. But the jobs that she could actually help him with were few and far between – even with all of her skills, Babylon's work was out of her league. All Aria had wanted to do was make a little bit of money with some mercenary work. It had been impossible to work once someone had started tailing them. She had almost thought it was that obscenely powerful Adept again, but Piano hadn't been able to feel an Adept aura on the person following them. It was either a highly skilled operative from Project Maestro or some mega-corp. She really hoped that it was an operative from Project Maestro trying to bring her in, she didn't need a would-be assassin from a mega-corp. If Project Maestro was the one behind this, she could take a small bit of comfort that they hadn't sent an Opus, someone like her.

Aria did have to wonder why Project Maestro was coming after her now. The first six months after she and Light had abandoned their duties had been hellish. Other Opera had been chasing after them, there had been government soldiers going after them, Project Maestro had even resorted to some freelance mercenaries from mega-corps. But after that magic six month point things had calmed down. Aria had gone off the grid entirely and Light had set up his fortress in Fairwind. It had been just over three years since they had left. The timing just didn't make sense.

Her food arrived and she ate it slowly. It had been awhile since she had last eaten and it was taking a toll on her body. Piano always got a little antsy when she didn't eat enough – he had always been quite protective of her. She ate and paid. She wanted to put the café as far behind her as she could. Aria kicked a piece of garbage out of her way while she walked out, her black trench coat twining around her legs. She and Piano needed to plug in and discuss things face to face. Plugging in gave a face to the disembodied voice in her head and made her feel less crazy for listening to the voice in her head. It helped the host and AI bond a bit more and learn to trust each other. Trust was very important when an AI could literally take over the host's body if they felt like it.

She squinted up at the sky for a moment before pulling her blue goggles over her eyes. The sky was burnt to an angry orange color and the tendrils of the sun's rays were an eerie red. The sky had been that color since before she was born. She had heard that the sky had been a beautiful and bright blue during the day, and a blue so dark that it was nearly black at night. The only time she saw sky like that was when she was in Night City, which was quite literally, a different world. Books told her that stars were visible before the attacks. Aria's stomach knotted painfully – thinking of the damaged sky did that to her. Once the sky had been scarred, the strict laws on citizens had been put in place. While she disagreed with a lot of the laws, she had been forced to accept them or face the government's wrath. She sure as hell didn't want to go to one of the camps.

"Piano, we should really plug in. It's been a long time since we've had the chance and we really need to figure out what we're going to do about this. I miss you."

"I was about to suggest the same thing, it'll help us get everything planned out. I'm setting a course."

"Come out of the city for work and I'm getting tailed by an operative..." Aria mumbled in her mind. *"Makes more sense now, doesn't it? They either wanted us distracted enough that we didn't notice the wanted poster, or they wanted to send a message. Either way, it's not a good thing. Here I thought we might actually have luck this time."*

"Murphy's Law."

Aria managed to laugh a little at that. Murphy's Law defined almost all their trips outside of Night City, anything that could go wrong usually went wrong. She reached up and tugged at her hair. The pink looked like fire in the harsh orange light. She was going to have to change it. Again. She hated changing her appearance, but she knew it was a necessarily evil of someone in her position. The operative had managed to get a glimpse of how she looked and that meant that she was obligated to change. She reached down and tapped a button on the side of her skates and sighed. Her life was change and it was time to continue forward.

CHAPTER 2

Aria groaned as she ran a hand through her newly cropped, black hair. Her hair had been almost waist length, now it barely brushed her shoulders. She was certain that black was an awful color for her, but she had wanted something very different than pink. Black would help her blend in. She had a cache of different colored contacts for occasions like this; she had put in a pair that made her eyes look like gold. They wouldn't help her blend in, but she was willing to chance having odd colored eyes. Her own eyes were a very distinct blue-green.

She and Piano could not go back to Project Maestro. She had a decent amount of cash left, but she had left Night City so she could generate some income. When Aria was at Project Maestro, they had taught them that the economy had crashed once the skies had been burned. The government had lost a great deal of control over its people as well. Larger cities and areas surrounding them still followed the laws that the government had put in place. Small cities were free and oftentimes more terrifying than the government-run cities. The lack of structure had reduced several small cities to havens for the worst kind of people.

Aria had been their first success in the field of humans being implanted with artificial intelligence units. She tried not to think of it too often; Project Maestro had ripped her away from her family when she was only thirteen years old, under the guise of a school for highly gifted children. She hadn't seen her younger sister Madeline, or her parents, since then.

She and Piano needed to plug in and talk face to face and plan their actions carefully. Three years hiding from Project Maestro had taught her to be cautious. She was hoping that there would be a sketchy LAN café around, but most of them had been destroyed by the government, the ones left were from the golden age. Every once and awhile she had enough luck to stumble onto one of them. Smaller settlements had remnants of LAN cafes; this town might be too big or too close to a major city. But any computer would due, she and Piano would be able to plug in then.

"Piano, do you feel any computer signals in this area?"

"I'm working on it. I'm trying to be discrete in case we have some stalkers."

All Project Maestro AIs had been given the ability to remotely access the internet and other various sources. Aria wasn't quite sure how it worked, just that it was a bonus that came with having another consciousness in her mind. Even after ten years of Piano she didn't know all of his features. She doubted that she would ever know all of his features.

"Looks like the closest computer is in this upcoming 'office building'. The one on the right."

Aria glanced at the building and blanched. The building had bars on the windows and numerous bullet holes in every window. She could see that the foundation of the building was crumbling a bit. It looked like it was only standing because the building itself was stubborn. She couldn't afford to be picky about where they plugged in. The front door was sealed shut with steel – she grumbled – she knew that it would be military grade and that there was no way of using her tiny knife that was made of some sort of plasma to get through. She walked through a narrow alley to the side of the building and was delighted to see a rusted ladder barely hanging on to the wall. She could hear Piano protesting in the back of her mind and ignored him. He always got a little over-protective of her when she could possibly hurt herself. Her body was his home, if she died, he died.

"Don't worry, I'll be sure to slice my hand on every rung."

"Very funny. Did you know that tetanus shots aren't available to the general public anymore? I'm pretty sure that yours is out of date. Please be careful."

Aria reached up and grabbed the lowest rung and climbed up until her feet could touch a rung. She felt her left hand slip as the flesh tore. Wincing, she stepped up onto the equally rusted platform, hoping that her weight wouldn't cause it to collapse. The only entrance was a murky glass window. She stepped back a little and kicked her foot through the window. She was glad that glass had been brittle. Aria stepped through the window carefully, thankful that she was flexible. She was mindful of the jagged glass that rimmed the window frame. The floor had a thick layer of dust that swirled around her feet as she took steps. It was clear that this building hadn't been inhabited in years. She glanced around the room and saw the computer leaning crooked in the corner.

"Haven't seen one that old in a long time," Aria said as she approached it. *"Are you sure it's functional?"*

Internet and computers weren't forbidden – but they were very hard to come by. Especially in smaller towns like this. An Opus made do with what they found. On official missions most were given a portable internet source or a small laptop to make things easier.

"There's a signal coming off of it."

She ran her hands over the case and found a large crack running down the left side, still, she figured it would be in working condition unless water had managed to leak in over the years. She sat down into the dust and reached up to the back of her neck where there was a nondescript scar that was about two inches in length. Aria shuddered at the feeling of the long cord slipping out of her neck, she didn't look at it – she knew it was coated with blood. They called it a bio cord at Project Maestro. She reached and plugged the cord into the back of the computer.

The familiar sensation of electricity flooded through her body and she welcomed it like an old friend. She had learned years earlier that fighting the electricity only led to being shocked or other painful situations. She had never really figured out how plugging in worked, just that the cord was a synthetic extension of her spinal cord and that allowed her to go into the realm of the AIs. The major downside to plugging in was that Aria's body was completely unresponsive the entire time. On the other hand, her digital self would be free to move and interact with Piano.

Within moments, the rushing stopped and she was in the electronic realm with Piano. His appearance always surprised her. He looked so young. When he spoke within her mind, he always sounded much older than her. Even when she was a confused thirteen year old, Piano had looked the same; hair that was such a dark brown that it looked like it was nearly black and pale green eyes. He had never aged the entire time she had known him. She shivered for a moment, shaking away the last of the electric feeling that crawled over her skin. She glanced around the realm – it was so different than what she was used to. Everything was bleached out and buzzing with an electric current. Even Piano's clothing was partially whited out; she could only tell that it was darker in coloration.

"Good to see you, Piano," Aria said as she stretched her arms above her head, her face twisted in amusement as she noticed that her hair was both pink and waist length. The digital realm had restored it.

He inclined his head, sending his nearly black hair tumbling from its neat position, "And you as well. It's been way too long," his face softened for a split second, before firming into stone. "Each time we leave Night City to come and earn some money, our position gets more compromised. We need a safe house, or we need to go back."

"I'd agree to go back, but I don't want to bring our trouble over," Aria hated jumping straight into business. "Night City has enough problems without us bringing over any of ours. So, the real question is who do we bug?"

There was a small silence between the two of them.

"What about Allegro?" Piano said.

"...Allegro is an AI."

"I'm aware of that. His host is acceptable."

Light Morrison was Allegro's host. He had been one of the first people Aria had met at Project Maestro. They had a very sibling-like friendship, screaming at each other one moment, saving each other from certain death at other times. With Jean Thomas 'Jinto' Jameson they had been a three-man infiltration team. Eventually they had escaped Project Maestro together – Jinto had stayed at Project Maestro to act as an informer and to keep them safe. While they were friends, they were prone to arguing more than getting along unless Jinto was with them.

"Last time we saw Light and Allegro, they explicitly asked that we stay away for a bit unless they asked for help. He seems to think we bring trouble with us and I really have to agree with him. He might end up hurting us if we show up."

"They said if we really needed help, we could go there. Do we have any other choices?"

"He only said that because Allegro made him!"

Aria took a few steps away from Piano. She glanced at the ground, every once and awhile she thought she could see grass that had circuitry running through it, but the second she saw it, it disappeared. She sighed; she knew that Piano was right, she just didn't want to admit it yet. She really didn't want to bring trouble onto Light.

She turned back to him, her face scrunched up as she said, "I don't like this."

"I know, but it's our safest choice."

She glowered at Piano for a moment before letting her face soften into a smile, "I guess it really is our safest choice."

"I'm plotting our best path to Fairwind now."

Project Maestro was in the Midwest, near Minnesota used to be. Fairwind was on the east coast, closer to where New Jersey used to be. Light had wanted to get far away from Project Maestro without going too far south. The further south a person went the worse the skies got.

"Alright, I'm going to unplug then. This area makes me nervous."

Aria wrapped her arms around Piano and felt him tense for just a moment. She knew that the

15

physical contact startled him every time, but his arms slipping through her vibrant, pink hair told her that he appreciated it. It showed that they were just as connected as they were when Piano had originally entered Aria's consciousness. And with that, she unplugged herself from the computer. Aria closed her eyes in pain – while plugging in was a glorious feeling if done properly, unplugging was unpleasant in every way. She equated it to a bad migraine, including the light sensitivity and the not wanting to move part. She groaned as she rubbed at her eyes. Her skin was coated in a fine sheen of cold sweat.

"Aria, are you alright?"

"Yeah...I don't think I'll ever get used to that..."

Even after ten years, she doubted that she would get used to the sensation of unplugging. She pushed herself off of the ground, brushing the thick dust from her pants and trench coat. She clamped a hand over her eyes as she leaned against the computer desk with her other hand. Aria knew that the pain would disappear in a few minutes, she just disliked being disoriented while she was on the move.

"I'm going to guess that you want to travel by train?"

"Yeah, I'm too tired to make the skate to Fairwind," she said while making her way out of the building. They were currently in what used to be Maine.

Civilians had two choices for transportation: taking train or walking. Motor vehicles were reserved for military officials. Even then, use of motor vehicles was strictly monitored. The government had to try to preserve what was left of the skies, after all.

"We should leave soon, our train leaves in the next half an hour."

Aria grumbled as she yanked her goggles over her eyes. She tapped a button on the side to make them a darker shade of blue.

"Piano...take over. I'm not feeling that great."

She felt Piano meld into her limbs, like hot liquid running down each extremity. They had done this so many times that she didn't panic. She trusted her AI. Aria felt Piano push off with her leg while she tried to ease her pain away.

CHAPTER 3

Aria gazed up at the large building before her. It still boggled her mind that Light had decided to hide out in a mansion, but it had been smart. The place was monstrous and it had been very well fortified. Somehow he had managed to cloak the whole place from radars. He had been smart enough to forge an alliance with the Underground and had been able to build a passage.

"Is Light in? I can never tell."

"Yes, I've been chatting with Allegro. Let's just get this over with."

Aria walked up to the house and hit the call button. Light's paranoid voice demanded that she identify herself. She smiled a little. To ensure that they really knew it was Aria coming for help, they had set up a password.

"Want to go to the opera?"

She heard Light breathe in sharply, followed by the electronic hiss of the door opening. She entered the building apprehensively, taking in the bleak decor with a trained eye. Aria could tell that he was hiding weapons behind the antique grandfather clock that wasn't ticking. She would have to keep that in mind in case things went really sour.

Aria listened to the panicked footsteps pounding down the staircase and watched a flustered Light enter the room. She smiled involuntarily at his flushed face and wide eyes; he looked so much like he had when they had escaped. Light was a very attractive man, except for a nasty scar that ran from his right eyebrow down to the side of his mouth. His hair was a pleasant coppery color and his eyes were nearly golden, but still well within the range of brown. She glanced up at him and remembered times when she had been the taller one.

"Aria, is that you?"

She understood Light's confusion. She had looked quite a bit different the last time he had seen her. Her hair had been just past her waist and some random color of the rainbow. She wished that he had been able to see her hair when it was bright blue. It was understandable that her hair barely touching her shoulders would be a little confusing, much less her with black hair. She knew that Light understood how much she loved having colorful hair. In all the years that they had known each other, Aria had avoided dying her hair black.

"It's me," she said as she slipped her arm out of her trench coat and revealing the jagged scar that ran from her left shoulder to between her breasts. The only other scar that would have convinced him was the implantation scar on the back of her neck – and Aria didn't really feel like giving Light her back.

"Allegro tells me that he feels Piano. He wouldn't lie to me. What I'm really curious about is *why* the hell you're here."

Aria tucked her hands into the pockets of her trench coat and paced around a little bit before saying, "Have you been outside lately?"

"Not for a few days. I try to go out a bit every day, but you know how it goes. I just got back from a job a few days ago, so I've been resting."

"Well, I was checking the holoboard notices to see if I could get some mercenary work and I saw a wanted bulletin for me. I didn't stick around long enough to see if there was one for you."

Light's eyes narrowed into slits.

"I need to hide out for a few days; I had some operatives following me."

"And you want to bring them here?" Light said, balling his hands into fists. "You didn't find a bulletin for me. You don't know if they're after me. They're after you. I'm not going back after what we discovered."

"*I don't like where this is going, Piano.*"

"*I don't either. I'm working on escapes. Keep yourself on guard; you know how fast he is when he wants to be.*"

To an extent, the AI affected the host it was implanted in. It probably dealt more with compatible personalities. Personality was one of the most important criteria for implantation. Aria wasn't sure exactly why, but considering each AI had a different personality that reflected their name – it was important for Project Maestro to

20

consider compatible personalities. Regardless, Piano made Aria stealthy. Allegro made Light incredibly fast.

"I know they're after me, but they'll be after you too. In case you forgot, we're both Opera. We've both killed people," Aria took a deep breath and scuffed her boot against the floor. "Just give them a little bit of time."

Aria barely had any time to react as Light reached to the back of his pants and pulled out an energy gun. She whipped her messenger bag to the front of her body and grabbed a random knife. His gun was pressed to her chest while her knife was millimeters away from his neck. She knew that he had come in to close the distance because he was actually unwilling to shoot her. If he had meant to kill her he would have done so already.

"*Well, this has gone sour. How are his vitals looking?*"

"*Just a little bit of an understatement there,*" her AI snarked. "*He's in better health than you. Far better rested. You're a better fighter than him.*"

"*That doesn't necessarily mean anything.*" Aria had excelled in technique, but Light was a dirty fighter. Honor had no place in a fight.

She took a deep breath before she dropped her knife and disarmed Light's gun. He grabbed Aria's shoulder and shoved her against the wall, his other hand slamming into her gut. She gasped as the air escaped her lungs, but brought her knee into Light's gut. He tumbled to the ground, eyes squinted shut.

"Aria, get out of there!"

Aria turned her back on Light despite her training screaming in her mind that giving her back to her opponent was suicide. She started making her way towards the door; she needed to get out. She felt pressure above the small of her back and crashed into the wall. Spots danced in front of her eyes, she hoped that she didn't have a concussion. She rolled over onto her back and saw Light standing above her, his left arm holding his ribs and his other pointing the energy gun at Aria's face.

"I don't know what you're playing at, Aria, you're a huge hazard to my safety, but I'm not sticking my neck out for you," Light said as he grabbed her by the trench coat and pants and tossed her out the front door.

CHAPTER 4

Aria leaned back against the headboard of the bed. After Light had unceremoniously thrown her out of his fortress, she and Piano had hacked into a seedy motel's database and snagged a room. She had mowed down almost two plates of food. The shady hotel was similar to the ones they usually crashed in. The carpet was threadbare and stained with what looked like blood. It would be a good place to get her strength back and hide for a little bit. Her body ached in ways that it hadn't in a few months. She knew that there would be bruises coating her shoulder blades and her face. The shower had brought some of the bruises to the surface, which she was thankful for, that meant that they weren't bone bruises. Showering had always helped her calm her mind.

"*That could have gone better,*" Aria whispered as she set the plate to the side of her.

"*It opened his eyes; that's all we can really hope for.*"

Aria sighed, stretching her stiff arms out in front of her. She tensed; she could feel the uncomfortable heat of someone's eyes on her.

"*Piano, scan for AIs, please, something feels weird.*"

She slid off the bed onto her haunches, more feline than human for a moment. She closed her eyes, she knew that depriving one of her senses could strengthen the others, but no sounds came in stronger.

"I can feel an AI, but it's masking from me. Hate when they do that. Proceed with caution."

Aria nodded. Caution was necessary. If this was one of the operatives that had been following her, this was a much more dangerous situation than she was willing to think about. She jumped to her feet as she heard the soft scrape of fabric on the slick walls. Her hands flew to the switchblade that was stuffed in her boot as she pinned the intruder against the wall. Aria looked at her intruder; it was Light, pale and shaking.

"What the hell are you doing here?" Aria snapped, dropping him to the ground. "You know better than to sneak up on an Opus."

He stayed in a lump on the floor for a moment, his breathing ragged. She watched as he pushed himself to his feet, his body was shaking as he said, "They followed you to Fairwind. They followed you to my home."

Aria felt herself go pale - she had never meant to bring trouble to Light, she had just wanted some help. She had never meant to endanger what he had finally called home.

"What happened to your stronghold?"

"I detonated it – the bastards managed to get in. I don't think I got any of them with the blast, though," he paused for a second and fidgeted with the edge of his sleeves. "I couldn't let those bastards get to the Underground."

She hadn't even considered his passage to the Underground. Knowing Light, the passage had been very well hidden. It had been hard enough to barter help from them to start with – the Adepts had been able to sense the AIs. It would have been near impossible for someone with an AI to get help when being chased by highly skilled agents.

"*Still paranoid as ever,*" Aria said in her mind and then spoke to Light. "I assume you want my help?"

Aria strode back to the bed and plopped down onto it. She crossed her ankles and glanced over at Light. He looked less put together than he had back at his fortress. His coppery hair was clinging to his forehead from sweat, his face was flushed, and his own gray goggles were hanging around his neck. There were a few tears in his pants.

"I'm sorry about how I acted, you know how I get when I feel threatened," he said, the words seemed like they were measured with care. "It is ultimately your fault that the operatives came after me. I can't stay mad though, I know you only needed my help. I just don't know what to do...I don't get around as much as you do. I assume going to Night City is out of the question?"

Getting to Night City involved hopping a bus – which were hard enough to find in her horizon without the added stress of being chased. If the operatives were really so close behind them they might swarm the bus. And she couldn't help but think that one of them might be an Adept – she had already theorized that powerful Adepts would be able to go through the void between horizons, between universes. She couldn't let that happen. One day after hopping a bus Aria had found herself in Night City and had met Babylon. She had lived there on and off for two and a half years – if she could avoid bringing them trouble, she would do so.

"Yes, it is. I don't want anything from this universe following us over there. But if we're leaving, we're leaving soon. And we're playing by my rules. I didn't think that the operatives were so close behind me," she said, her voice taking on a professional tone that she sometimes hated.

"I agree. It would be foolish to stay in this area."

She noted that Light's voice had taken on the same tone and suppressed a smirk. Aria winced as Piano slapped her mind. He rarely did that - he reserved it for times when he was exceptionally angry with her or needed to get something across.

"Piano, you know we have to!"

"I am aware that the operatives are in this area, but you are in no condition to start running again. You need to get your strength back."

She looked over at Light, whose face was pulled down in a frown. She assumed that he was getting an earful from Allegro.

"I'm going to go ahead and think that both of our AIs are saying that we shouldn't run?"

Light scoffed, "Allegro says that you're nowhere near full strength and that his scan says you're getting sick with something."

Aria furrowed her brow. Getting sick wasn't in the cards. She could only hope that she had some bug from Night City and not what plagued her realm; scorched atmosphere lung toxicity. The disease had started cropping up about six months after the skies had been burnt - at least that was what Aria had read. Most people spent so much time indoors that the disease wasn't a huge deal – but to the poorer people of the former United States it was basically a death sentence.

"I told you that you needed to rest. We should all plug in. This is far too important for us to discuss like this, plus, it's been ages since I've seen Allegro, much less any AI."

Aria looked around the room, she had remembered seeing a computer when she and Piano had commandeered the room, but hadn't noticed how modern it was – modern computers were a rarity in seedy motels. It was a small chrome silver box with several ports and a holoboard, small, but perfect for what they needed. She motioned for Light to follow her. She started to pull the long cable from the back of her neck, shuddering at the sensation. Light did the same. Plugging in with two hosts worked just the same as with one host, they were plugged into the same source, therefore they would be able to communicate.

The electricity engulfed her and she found herself in the bleached realm of the AIs. A smile spread across her face as Light popped into the realm, his face looking politely confused. Everyone reacted to the transfer to the digital realm differently.

"Hello boys," Aria said while walking over to Piano.

Allegro blended in with the realm; his white blonde hair and pale complexion was a natural camouflage against the buzzing walls. He inclined his head at Aria, "Been ages since I've seen you Aria, you've grown up."

They stood in slightly awkward silence before Aria said, "Running is the best option and both of you know it. We can't stay in Fairwind any longer. Not with the operatives there."

Light nodded in agreement, "Allegro and I felt something really off about those operatives."

Piano shifted uncomfortably, "I could tell they had AIs, but they felt different than any of the Opera AIs."

The silence fell again. The humming and buzzing of the walls and floor was nearly deafening.

It was Allegro who broke the silence this time, "Look, Aria, Light, I know you guys are right about this. We all need to run, but neither of you are in the best condition for running. Piano and I are just concerned."

"I appreciate the concern but I'm fi-"

"Aria, unplug. Now."

The tone in Piano's voice snapped her away from train of thought. She looked around the realm; both Allegro and Light were missing. Panicked, she unplugged and gasped as she surfaced back into the real world. She fought through the disorientation and stood to see Light on the ground bleeding from the back of his neck. She couldn't see him breathing.

"Is the assailant still here?"

"Yes, I can feel him...and his AI."

Aria could hear shuddering breathing in the small corridor that led to the door. A feral grin passed over her face, the operative hadn't expected them to react so quickly. Aria looked around the corner and saw the operative, dark haired with pale skin, leaning against the wall, gasping for breath. He seemed to be muttering under his breath into a watch. While he was still distracted with that, she sidled up next to him and grabbed his shoulder firmly. A small squeak escaped the man's lips. He was far too mousy to be an Opera. Too timid. He seemed lost and confused – those weren't good traits for an assassin and infiltration expert.

"Who are you?" she demanded.

"Diminuendo."

"Not your AI. Who are you?"

"Diminuendo."

"Piano, what's up with him?"

"He's telling the truth, I can't feel any lies off of him."

Aria let her breath out slowly - she shouldn't let the little pipsqueak get her frustrated, even if he had injured Light.

"Did Project Maestro send you?" The man looked away from her, toward the door. It seemed that he was seriously contemplating running. She backhanded him across the face, a startled gasp issued from the small man. "Let's try this again. Did Project Maestro send you?"

He hesitated a moment before nodding. She narrowed her eyes, he had to be lying.

"Are you an Opus?"

He shook his head furiously but looked up at her with his piercing mercury eyes, "Always together, never to part, Fugue will finish what Opus starts..."

The operative shoved Aria in the sternum, sending the air flying from her lungs. He was small and quick and gone before she had a chance to regain her bearings. Gasping, she managed to pull herself to her knees. His quick escape told her that he was more there for information than anything. Had he been instructed to kill them or bring them back, the situation would have ended differently. Aria knew that was true, it had to be true.

"*Piano, dig up whatever you can on a Fugue Project or Project Fugue from the Maestro database. Thanks.*" At this point she didn't care about the risk. Her AI was smart enough to mask their presence.

Aria crawled back to where Light was curled up. One of his hands was on the back of his neck;

the other was clamped over his eyes. At least he was groaning, that meant he was alive. She had been worried that forced removal from the realm of AIs could have killed him.

"You alright, Light?"

"I'm alive...just the usual pain after coming back to our world, well, and some bleeding, but that'll heal over just fine," Light said, sarcasm dripping from his voice.

"*Aria, I can't find anything on Fugue in the Project Maestro database. Must be top secret - and they revoked your top secret privileges once you deserted.*"

"*Figured, was worth a shot anyways.*"

Aria helped Light up into a sitting position and cradled his body against her very lean body. She tried to lift him up onto the bed, but failed, both of them crashing back to the ground. Light groaned horribly, his brows furrowing together.

"I can't lift you," there was an edge of panic in her voice - she was supposed to be stronger than a normal person.

"No really...just leave me here. I'll be fine."

Aria listened to Light, but grabbed him a pillow and put his head on it. She sat down on the bed herself and lifted up her shirt to see her sternum, there was a dark bruise blossoming across her chest. She had been hit much harder than she had thought; bruises usually took a few hours to show up on her.

"Light, we have a problem. That guy...he's a lot stronger than I thought. We really do have to get out of here."

She heard him grunt, she assumed it was in agreement.

"Piano, do you agree now?"

"I do. This confirms that you have enhanced operatives following you though."

Aria nodded. She yawned. It had been an exhausting day. Fighting with Light, Light get injured, getting attacked by an operative. The operative had hesitated before saying he was from Project Maestro. She had to wonder if they were even involved in this. The holoboard was their style, but sending someone who would injure a bio-cord wasn't. The whole situation was far too complicated – she knew that they should be running but rest was needed first.

CHAPTER 5

Aria knew that she was dreaming, but she couldn't get herself to wake up. She looked at her surroundings and felt her heart start racing. The stark architecture could only mean one thing; she was in the Project Maestro facility.

"My Opera," a booming male voice said.

Aria's eyes widened into saucers, she didn't want to see him now, she never wanted to see Stratton. He was a tall man and had a wider frame as well. She didn't let his aged appearance fool her; he was still a formidable soldier and fighter. His hair was graying, but still mainly brown. His eyes were the type that she thought could have been nice at one point, but were so frosted over that they gave her goose bumps.

"Now that you've all had successful AI implantations, it's time to start training – "

"Training for what?" another of the Opus members, Holly, asked. She had plain brown hair and hazel eyes that were currently leveled at Stratton. There was a bit of fire in the girl's voice, a bit of challenge. "I thought this was a school for highly gifted and intellectual teenagers."

"You're training to be the United States' top assassins," Stratton finished, the corner of his mouth twitching with impatience. "The AI units we've implanted will improve your reflexes, will help you learn, and will increase your awareness by being your awareness. We will enhance your muscles and skeleton. You will be perfect assassins."

"But we're under-aged," a second Opus, Eric, said while playing with the drawstring of his pants. He was so thin that his pants barely stayed on his hips. His protest was foolish, in Aria's mind. She had the distinct feeling that the government would do whatever they wanted to do. "You can't make us learn how to kill people."

"And that's where you're all wrong. All of your parents gave you over to the government. I am your legal guardian and you will do as I say," Stratton paused for a moment, his eyes gleaming. "You're all very intelligent teenagers. You all know that I am just as smart and that I am stronger."

Aria looked over at Light and Jean Thomas (she had started calling him Jinto almost immediately), the two boys she had met on their first day at the Project Maestro facility. Light looked as he always did, surly. It was clear that this turn of events didn't sit well with him. Jinto, on the other hand, looked contemplative and curious.

"Even if you're our guardian, we're still under-aged. What about labor laws? What about child abuse?" Jinto asked, his hands open in front of him. A slightly better set of questions – but still, the government would do what they wanted. If they wanted children to learn how to kill, then children would learn how to kill.

Stratton motioned for all of the Opus members to stand up in order. Aria took her place at the head of the line, next to Jinto. Stratton paced along them looking them all dead in the eyes, trying to intimidate them. He made his way down the row, stopping at each one individually. Most of them held his gaze, but looked quite uncomfortable. Eric looked away, a frown etched on his face. When his icy blue eyes met her own blue-green, she felt her breath catch in her throat.

"What you seem to be forgetting is that the government bends rules in their projects. We needed developing brains, muscles, and bones, and the government delivered. I'm willing to bet the government isn't going to complain with how I treat you here," he paused long enough to make eye contact with all of them again. "You will do as I say. You will learn to infiltrate, you will learn strategy, you will learn to kill."

Aria gripped her fingers around Jinto's wrist. She closed her eyes and tried to hide the tears that were threatening to fall.

"Oh, is little Opus 1 scared?" Stratton said as he lifted her up by her left shoulder. "Don't worry little one, you're safe here." He tossed her to the ground while laughing.

Aria woke with a start. They were moving; Piano had to be in control. She glanced to her left; Light was with them, looking like he was in agony.

"*Piano?*" she asked, her mind was still a little fuzzy from the dream.

"*I'm here Aria. Your mind needed to rest, so I took over and let you sleep. I hope that's okay.*"

"*Don't worry about it. I'm just surprised. It's been a long time since I've fallen asleep when you were in control.*"

She looked around at their surroundings; dying trees and shattered mountains all on a platter of withered grass. They were far into the countryside.

"*I was surprised myself...you seldom remember dreams, even nightmares, what's special on this one?*"

"Stratton."

Aria didn't have to say anymore. When she had first arrived at Project Maestro, things had been alright. The seven original Opera had pretty much free reign of the facilities. She had been able to keep dancing and studying and it had made her happy. When Stratton had finally started the real Opus program, she had shattered, and he was the one who had wielded the hammer. He had made sure that each of the teenagers had become his pawns before he sent them on missions. She had only been thirteen, the oldest had been seventeen, when they found out their purpose.

"Glad to have you back with us," Light said, his face brightening a little bit.

"Glad to be back...what happened? I don't remember anything after sitting down on the bed."

"You were awake for a bit, but once we started moving and Piano took over...well...you were out."

"Why are we out in such a rural area?"

"Piano and Allegro figured it would be safer. We'll know if someone's coming for us."

Aria could see their logic, but it seemed flawed to her. No one ever came out this way, ever. There would be no building for them to hide in.

"Relax Aria, we did our research."

She wasn't very comforted, but she let herself relax a little. Normally, when Piano was in control, it was very easy for her to relax, hence, why she used to fall asleep while he was in control. She had built up a bit of a tolerance for that and as she was curious by nature, she was always watching what was going on. As she looked at the area around her, she noted that all the trees were scorched and withered, the grass was a yellow color, and the orange-grey sky made everything worse. This had to have been one of the sites that had been directly hit.

"Light...are you ok? Are you still able to reach Allegro?"

"Yeah. I don't think I'll be able to plug in for a while though. Hurts like hell when I try to pull the cord out. Allegro is still there though. He's pissed off at the operative."

Aria felt relieved. She couldn't imagine what life would be like without her AI and she imagined the same was true of Light. She felt mildly guilty that she was glad that Diminuendo had grabbed at Light's cord and not hers.

"Piano, want to let me have control? I want to feel the terrain."

She knew that Piano would let her have it reluctantly. She only fell asleep when very out of it; he would think it wasn't safe for her to be in control of her own body. She felt him relinquish control slowly, easing her into control. Her eyes adjusted to the dull sunlight that was illuminating everything with an eerie orange glow. Everything looked like it was on fire. Then the pain came. Her legs were weak and her chest was killing her. Grimacing through it, she brought her goggles down over her eyes and tapped a second button that allowed her to zoom in scan for other life forms. This place truly was deserted.

"What do you think of this place, Aria?"

"Seems...quaint. Even a little small for me. I guess my warehouse idea was shot down?"

"Yeah...a little bit. The guys after us seem to understand how you like warehouses and how I prefer my safe house."

The operatives. Fugue. She remembered what a fugue was from when she was a dancer, from when she was younger. It was a multi-voice theme in a composition, she had never really danced to one, but they were awesome to listen to. She knew it meant that there was more than one operative, but that was all she could figure out. In terms of an operative, it just didn't make sense to be called Fugue. The Opus project had produced assassins and spies that could work together or apart. They were each a complete work, but they could work together if need be. The idea of Fugue just confused her.

She and Light came to a small, clearly abandoned shack. There were scorch marks going up and down the sides, like someone had taken a flamethrower to it. Aria glanced at Light and he shrugged, discomfort all over his face.

"Home sweet home." Aria said, opening the door slowly.

CHAPTER 6

Aria rested her head back against the rough wall of the shack. She reached into her messenger bag and pulled out some dried meat that she had picked up at a checkpoint awhile back. She offered some to Light, who shook his head. The isolation let her mind wander too much. It let her think about how much she missed Night City, how much she missed Babylon. She had left the city a few months earlier to earn some money. She had only intended to be gone for, at maximum, a month. About two weeks in to her trip, operatives had started tailing her. She had been running since.

"Not like you to be lost in thought, Aria," Light said as he stretched his arms above his head.

"It's just so isolated."

"Says the girl who lives in abandoned warehouses and seedy hotels."

"This is different and you know it. The isolation is messing with my head."

Aria preferred staying in cities because there were resources. A shack in the middle of nowhere had no resources. It made her nervous. But the others were right – this wasn't a logical move. It might throw whoever was following them off their trail.

"*You know this was the best choice. The operatives clearly know our preferences,*" Piano said, he was attempting to make his voice sound like it usually did, calming. "*This was the only thing we could think of that would throw them off of our trail.*"

Aria knew that Piano was right. The operatives had caught her trail so quickly and she was positive that they had been staking outside of Light's fortress for quite a while. They knew their preferences and it simply didn't make sense. When she had been a working Opus she had stayed in quality housing – she worked for the government and they took care of their own. She had only been running for six months when she had made it to Night City. She hadn't been making good decisions at that point. There had been a few nights that she had slept on the street. How Fugue knew so much about their current preferences baffled her – as far as she knew, Project Maestro didn't have information on the decisions they had been making after those first six months.

Aria watched Light's entire body tense, his mouth formed a narrow line. He crawled towards her and motioned for her to be quiet. The atmosphere of the shack shifted from casual to charged.

He flattened his back against the wall and leaned over to Aria to whisper, "We have a problem. Four incoming adversaries. Two male, two female."

Aria closed her eyes slowly, she hadn't expected them to catch up so quickly, "Noted. Two for each of us?"

"I don't know if we should fight them, Aria, there are more of them and neither of us is in condition to fight. At least that's what Allegro is telling me."

"I'm aware that both of us are a little under optimum fighting shape, however, we were taught to fight in any condition. Remember that day they were testing how fast our bodies metabolize alcohol by making us spar continuously for five hours?"

She heard Light laugh and she smiled a little. That had been one of the most amusing memories from Maestro. Of course, being so thin, she had been beaten horribly for five hours straight, but it had been an interesting time. Now was not the time to be remembering humorous moments. She needed to be focused. She stood cautiously, her body pressed against the wall, and peered out the window. As Light had said, there were four people coming at them. They were coming fast enough to be there in less than a minute.

"*Piano, get ready, we're going to be fighting in about forty-five seconds.*"

Aria felt Piano's power buzz throughout her body, calming her nerves and strengthening her tired muscles. She glanced over at Light, his face still showed quite a bit of concern, but his posture was straighter, his body appeared relaxed. She thoroughly understood the concern. While an Opus was primarily trained to work as a solitary unit, they were deployed in groups. The individuals worked on independent projects that helped them complete the larger goal at hand. It was entirely bizarre for them to be fighting together without Jinto, the third member of their team.

Before she could really react, the flimsy door of the shack was breaking in. She felt Piano smooth her tattered nerves over and meld into her mind. Aria watched as the four operatives bowled into the shack and examined them carefully. They ran the gamut of size, which meant they would be varied in how they fought. She sneaked in a look at Light and fought back the urge to smirk at how his face was twisted in displeasure. She knew that he was thinking approximately the same thing. He caught her eye and she saw that gleam that all Opera got before a fight.

Aria was caught off guard by the first that connected with her jaw. Her head collided with the rickety wall and stars danced in front of her eyes. There was no hesitation between that and the next hit. She gasped as the hit glanced her ribs and dug up underneath. Her lungs burned as she forced air into them. She needed to turn the fight to her favor – if she kept taking hits she would lose quickly.

"*Piano, where are they weak?*" Aria said as she parried a punch.

Being able to gain input from her AI in the middle of a fight was something she was infinitely grateful for. It could easily turn the tide of a battle.

A few moments later, Piano said, "*Right now they're trying to do as much damage as they can. They're hitting hard, but they're hitting slow.*"

That was all she needed to know. It still wasn't a good situation, but she had an inkling on how to win. She shoved her attackers away and slid into an easy defensive stance. Piano guided her motions; a takedown here, a kick there. Soon enough she felt like she was out of the weeds.

A scream from Light pulled Aria's attention to him. Diminuendo, that damnably speedy operative from earlier, was latched onto Light's back. His female attacker was throwing vicious strikes to his face and abdomen. Aria made a move to assist him, but Light took things into his own hands. He clamped onto Diminuendo's arm and threw him into the female assailant with a roar.

The slight distraction put Aria on the defensive again. It only took her a moment to realize that she was only fighting one of her operatives. She felt her blood freeze as cold fingers clamped around her throat. Her eyes shut in terror.

"*Aria, don't give up!*" Piano said, his voice hitting his equivalent of yelling.

Her mind snapped into gear as Piano's consciousness melded with hers. They moved as one, nimbly dealing with the large blonde male that had grabbed her throat. She looked over to Light, he was pinned on the ground by two operatives. A cold hand clamped on her arm as she watched a third operative pile on top of him, one of the ones that she was supposed to be dealing with. She stared the blonde man in the eyes and kicked him with her strongest roundhouse, sending him flying into the threatening-to-fall-over wall. She looked over at Light one more time before bolting from the house. She knew that she couldn't save him. Not this time.

It had been Light's idea originally that if they were in a situation like this that they would go separate ways. No matter what. It wouldn't do any good for them to both be caught. It didn't make the inevitable decision any easier.

"Piano, what are we going to do?"

Tears were running down her face. She couldn't stop them. She had abandoned one of her best friends to save herself. She was completely disgusted with how she behaved – even if they had both agreed years before that this was the best choice.

"We're going to keep running."

And she did.

CHAPTER 7

It had been two days since Aria had abandoned Light to Fugue. She hadn't stopped running yet. She hadn't stopped to eat or sleep, she had simply kept running. She had needed to get away from her failure. She and Piano had barely spoken.

"Piano, we need to find somewhere to go. We've done an awful lot of running...my body aches and I'm very tired."

The fact that she was admitting anything was a sign. She had done missions while ill, while injured, while recovering from either of the former. If she was admitting to being tired, something was wrong.

"We're pretty close to Orpheus Ridge. I'll set a route."

Orpheus Ridge was one of their favorite cities to hide out in; though she didn't go very often. It had been almost a year since she had visited – between the running from operatives and living in Night City, she hadn't made her way there in quite some time. It was on the east coast – also in what used to be New Jersey. She loved that their Underground had a large amount of black market technology. While technology was pretty easy to get a hold of, the government frowned upon the general populace having the higher end items. Aria's roller blades and goggles were precious commodities, which she knew, and she treasured them. Normal people weren't able to afford electric roller blades and her goggles were different than the standard variety the government issued to the populace.

"*Sounds good.*"

Aria slowed down to a walk and reached down to activate her roller blades by tapping the button on the side. She had thought about using her electric roller blades when she had been running away from Fugue, but had ultimately decided against it. She wanted to put as much distance as possible between her and Fugue, her roller blades would leave deep grooves in the loose earth. She glanced back over her shoulder and let herself smile; her tracks were blowing away in the wind. Her choice had been smart.

Jagged towers that spewed smog jutted into the air; they marked the perimeter of the city. It comforted her to see broken buildings on the close horizon, it meant that she was getting closer to a safe place. A safe house for her and Piano. Her breath caught for a moment, she had forgotten that the city had a checkpoint. She would have to show identification to get in. She abruptly stopped skating and started rummaging through her messenger bag. She had to wonder if she had an ID that showed her eyes as golden. The last time she had gone through a checkpoint her hair had been pink. She plucked one out and felt her breathing start again. Today she was Jessica Moore, age eighteen.

As she took in a deep breath of smog, she felt her lungs spasm, a cough ripping through her throat. Aria always reacted to the thick smoke that billowed around the factory perimeter of Orpheus Ridge, but it was rarely this bad. She gasped for breath and leaned against a charred tree, wheezing.

"Aria, are you alright?"

"No, I don't think so. Do you think the rural air could have done this?"

The silence in her mind confirmed that she was just being foolish in guessing that.

"Run a diagnostic scan, please. We need to rule out scorched atmosphere lung toxicity."

"On that."

She closed her eyes and kept leaning on the remains of the tree. Contracting the disease would almost certainly be a death sentence. The government had originally called it scorched atmosphere tuberculosis, but had quickly discovered that the only way it acted like tuberculosis was that it made the person cough until they died. It also hadn't taken them very long to figure out that the toxins from the scorched sky were causing the disease. Gas masks weren't particularly helpful – the government hadn't been able to create one that filtered the toxins from the air properly.

"Aria...the scan indicates that you have it..."

She opened her eyes and glanced up at the orange sky and exhaled. One horrible thing after another.

"*Well, it's a good thing we're in Orpheus Ridge, we need to go see Miranda.*"

Miranda was a powerful Adept that Aria had met during one of her trips to Orpheus Ridge . They had been running from an operative from some megacorp that had recognized her as what she was. She had still been working for the government and Stratton at that point in time. They had found a small hiding spot and planned to stay there until the operative had left – but she found them first. She was a deaf woman with limited speech – they had communicated through notes. During one of Aria's last visits, they had discussed Miranda's past at a facility called Oculus Mentis – a place where unstable Adepts were kept safe. Miranda had been kept there because most Adepts that manipulated greater sciences had a touch of instability in them. She had escaped during a catastrophic incident a few years before Aria had started running.

She didn't need to say another word. Piano knew that she couldn't keep skating at this point, not with her wheezing so bad that she was getting dizzy. He took over for her and had her start towards the checkpoint.

Aria watched as they approached the checkpoint, nervous despite having ID. There were quite a few people in front of them; all had identical looks of defeat tinged with fear. No one liked having to go through a checkpoint. Each of the people in front of her got into the city without a second thought. To an extent, Aria could feel Piano showing her fake ID to guards. She watched their faces cloud with recognition for a moment.

"Doesn't she look a bit like that wanted poster?" one of the guards said to the other, his eyes narrowed in suspicion.

Aria tensed, she knew that she didn't need to tell Piano to be ready to run if they needed to. She felt Piano keep her muscles loose and relaxed.

"A little, but her hair and eyes are wrong. She's too young to be the one in question. The girl they're after is around twenty-three," he paused for a second, eying her a little more closely. "Sweetheart, we're letting you in, but get a better ID. You're not eighteen, you're sixteen at best."

"Will do, sir!" Piano said with Aria's voice.

"Welcome to Orpheus Ridge, Jessica Moore."

"*That was a little too close for comfort, but I'm flattered that I still look like I'm sixteen.*"

"*I agree on it being too close. This is where I wish you were an Adept who could mask her appearance...it would be so helpful at this point.*"

"*I thought that Project Maestro decided that implanting an AI into an Adept wouldn't work?*"

Piano's silence meant that she was right.

They walked through the streets, taking in their surroundings. Orpheus Ridge had been the crown jewel of the new government at some point in time. Now it was pretty much like everything else – falling apart. She noticed it wasn't uncommon to see someone leaning against the wall, blood trickling from the corner of their mouth. Everyone looked completely and utterly defeated. The city had really gone down the tubes since Aria had last visited.

Miranda's hiding place was buried beneath an old building that had once been a free clinic. Being mainly underground protected her hide-away from the government and any scavengers that might try to get in. It was even difficult for Aria to find. Piano lifted up the keypad and punched in the entrance code. She heard a few locks click out of place and the door slid open.

Miranda stood before them, throwing her arms around Aria, instantly recognizing her despite the make-over, most likely because she was an Adept. Intelligent brown eyes glanced over Aria's frame and realized there was something seriously wrong. She pulled Aria into the room and placed a hand on her forehead and widened her eyes in panic. She grabbed a piece of paper and scrawled out "When did you contract it?" Aria grabbed the paper "I don't know...I started coughing this morning." Miranda ran a hand through Aria's hair and made her sit down on an upturned crate.

Miranda opened her mouth to start speaking, but flapped her arms a little, then paced around the room a little. After this, she took a breath and started speaking, "Aria...I don't know if I can cure that. I can make it better for the time being, but curing it might be impossible." Her voice was marred by a thick speech impediment brought on by her deafness.

Aria felt her jaw drop, she didn't want to have this disease forever. But she understood Miranda's dilemma. The disease would only get worse unless she could get the irritants out of Aria's lungs, which was practically impossible. There was a great chance of doing harm rather than good when an Adept did something so invasive, especially if they hadn't attempted it before. She nodded anyway, cursing internally.

"Aria, are you okay?"

"Yeah, I'll be fine."

Aria didn't particularly enjoy lying to Piano; she knew that he could see through the lies, for the most part. But every once and awhile it was necessary for her to do so. She felt him buzz in her mind; it was something that he did when she was upset. She thought it felt similar to an animal curling up at her side. It was always welcome. Things had fallen apart when she had run away from Project Maestro. Every once and awhile she caught herself wondering why she had been stupid enough to flee; then she remembered what she, Light, and Jinto had discovered. Then she remembered there was a reason that she was never going back.

CHAPTER 8

Hot...everything was so very hot. Aria opened her eyes and felt sweat dripping down her forehead. She couldn't tell if she was awake or sleeping. She tried to look around, but felt the sweat slip into her open eyes and burn. Her head felt like it was stuffed full of molten lead; so hot and so heavy.

"No, don't move, Aria. You have a very high fever," Miranda's thick voice came from somewhere above her.

Groaning, Aria saw the blurry outline of Miranda and said, "W-what happened? I was fine...the last thing I remember is the two of us talking about my...my chances."

"You spiked a fever about a day ago and fell unconscious not long after. I kept you asleep to help with the healing and plugged you into a computer so I could better communicate with Piano...it's difficult to communicate with an AI when the person is unconscious. Things are going to get worse before they get better."

Aria lost her tenuous grip on lucidity and fell back into the deep sleep.

"I will *not* learn how to fight!" Aria screamed at Stratton while being held back by two guards.

"*Aria, please remain calm,*" Piano said.

Aria flinched at the voice in her mind, she liked it, but she wasn't near used to it yet. She had only had Piano for a few days; but she liked him a lot. She had been pretty suspicious when they said they would be receiving a bio AI. She had been especially suspicious because she hadn't been able to figure out the difference between a bio AI and a standard AI unit. The best answer she had gotten was that a bio AI unit latched straight onto the nervous system of a person while a standard AI unit had to be implanted into an exoskeleton. A lot of her doubts had been in the fact that AI units were usually used in combat situations. The excuse of a 'study guide' had been absolutely ridiculous.

"You are part of a government funded program. You will learn how to fight. You will do as you are told."

She had known that there was something off about Project Maestro. She hadn't been able to wrap her mind around the reasoning why the government would spend millions of dollars they didn't really have on creating a facility for a school. And then spending the same amount of money on creating AI units for each of the teenagers. Again, the reasoning the government and Stratton had fed them seemed ridiculous at best.

"No, I won't. I'm a dancer!" Aria struggled against the guards.

Stratton raised an eyebrow at her and grabbed her wrist.

Aria gasped in pain; she was curled on her side, it felt like her internal organs were melting. She felt a cool compress press against her forehead and she shivered violently before coughing. Something hot and sticky was coating her hands and she had the distinct feeling it was blood, but she was in too much pain to open her eyes.

"Piano?"

"I'm here with you..." His voice sounded weaker than she had ever heard.

"Are we going to make it through this?"

Piano buzzed in her mind, although it was weak, it was enough to make her relax.

A punch side-swiped across her face and then she was on the ground, groaning in pain. She still hadn't perfected her safe backward fall and had ended up bouncing her head on the floor. She felt a comforting buzz from her AI and felt him numb the pain in her face. She glanced up and was face to face with Jinto, who wore a look of worry.

"Are you alright, Aria? Normally you're a little more aware than this," he said while offering her a hand.

"Do not help her up, Opus 2. An Opus must be able to stand on their own," Stratton growled, slapping Jinto's hand away.

"With all due respect, sir," Jinto said, he nearly spit the word 'sir' out. "We aren't on a mission. And she's a thirteen year old girl, not an Opus."

"She is Opus 1, you are Opus 2. You will do as we say," with that, Stratton kicked Jinto in the stomach, doubling him over and sending his glasses flying into a corner.

Aria screamed as one of her hands flew to cover her gaping mouth. She rushed and grabbed Jinto's glasses before they could be stepped on. The entire time she glared up at Stratton. She felt Jinto put his weight on her arm and push himself to a standing position.

She had the distinct feeling that Stratton's harsh personality had a direct connection to the fact that General Crawford was standing in the doorway to the training facility. His arms were crossed over his chest, a smirk on his face. It almost looked like he wanted Stratton to fail. Aria knew that it was important for the government to be careful with this project – they had taken children from their families. Their families would not be pleased if their children died. Stratton was especially in a delicate position – it's not like he could just kill a kid to set an example.

"You need to accept that not everyone will bend to your will immediately. You're dealing with teenagers, not soldiers. At that, perhaps you will learn to take personality into consideration. None of us want to be here."

Aria opened her eyes; the pain was almost gone. She was wrapped up in soft, worn blankets and she could feel that Miranda had given her an IV. There was only so much that the woman could heal and dehydration wasn't one of them. She heard a thunderbolt and cursed inwardly; the rain made the irritants more prevalent.

"Piano?"

"I'm here. How are you feeling?"

"Better, not one hundred percent. I don't think I can move yet; but I'm not in as much pain anymore. Where's Miranda?"

"She's out trying to replenish her food stocks and her medical supplies. Said she'd be back here soon."

Aria was glad that Piano and Miranda had been able to communicate while she had been out. As far as she could gather, when she was plugged in while she was already unconscious, her mind stayed in her body, but Piano could be 'messaged' through the computer.

Aria heard locks clicking and hoped that it was Miranda and not anyone breaking in. She wasn't in any state to be fighting people off – she didn't even know if she could move. She listened carefully to the shuffling gait, unable to determine if it was Miranda. She felt a gentle hand touch her shoulder and a yell of joy.

"Aria! You're awake!" Miranda's muffled voice said.

Aria reached for a piece of paper and wrote out, 'how long was I out?'

"About a week. You've been in and out of consciousness and I nearly lost you a couple of times...but you'll be alright in the long run. I only managed to halt the disease. It could relapse."

Aria nodded, she had trouble believing it, but knew that Miranda would never lie to her. The disease was essentially a death sentence. A friend of hers had contracted it when she was little; the girl hadn't made it very long. She tried to move her head so she could see Miranda and her vision swam and crossed. Groaning, she closed her eyes tightly.

"I also suggest that you not move around too much; you've had a rough week. I'm surprised you didn't contract it earlier. Traveling in and out of this Horizon probably aggravated it."

It surprised Aria that Miranda used the term Horizon. No one used that term in this universe – it was a term that she had picked up in Night City.

Aria nodded slowly while she opened her eyes again. She felt better, but the idea of the disease relapsing didn't sit well with her. That made her a ticking time bomb. It would be a way to track her and that made her feel more vulnerable than she cared to admit.

"Piano, I had a dream about Jinto."

"Ahh, Jinto and Andante. I miss them. I wish they had come with us."

"You know as well as I that Jinto stayed behind to keep us safe. If we all vanished, it would seem like we had discovered something. Him going back made it look less suspicious. He's always been so good at strategy."

"Fair enough. Rest up, Aria. Will you at least listen when I say that now?"

"Might start doing that; it could prove to be useful."

Piano buzzed happily in her mind and she smiled. The dreams that she had been having disturbed her, but the image of Jinto calmed her. He had been one of her closest friends at Project Maestro, he was pretty much the exact opposite of Light. She missed him. She was sure that Piano missed Andante as well; they had gotten along quite well. Then again, she didn't know of any AIs that Piano didn't get along with.

Miranda brought Aria food, smiling broadly. Aria ate it quietly – she knew that they would have to leave Miranda's hideout soon. They were jeopardizing her safety; she knew that Miranda was on the list of people that Opera were supposed to subdue and bring back to the government. At least she wasn't on the kill list, well, she wasn't the last Aria had seen the kill list. While what she, Light, and Jinto had learned had been the main reason for her running away, the kill list had been another one. The kill list had anything from people who just knew too much to innocent Adepts who had managed to escape Oculus Mentis. She was Stratton's biggest success and failure all wrapped into one.

Aria grabbed another piece of paper and wrote, "Will I need a mask? I don't want anyone to get sick because of me."

Miranda stared at the paper for a moment and then at Aria, "I think you'll be fine without it.

You've already contracted scorched atmosphere...the smog will irritate it, but you should be fine without a mask. I can tell you want to leave soon...to keep me safe. I understand it. Just remember that you're always welcome."

Aria nodded blankly, it always freaked her out when Adepts looked into her mind. Aria was usually quite good at hiding her intentions. They would depart the next day, maybe they would stay in Orpheus Ridge for a little longer, there was no way that they had been found yet.

CHAPTER 9

Aria hated leaving Miranda, the woman was far too sweet for her own good. She needed to figure out why a Project Maestro group was out on their own – it seemed to her that they weren't operating under Stratton's orders. While Stratton was a bastard, he knew better than to injure the bio cord. She kicked at the ground, she still had to wonder why Project Maestro was pursuing her again; they hadn't seriously chased after her for a year or so. She couldn't figure out what was so special this time. Aria shook her head; it wasn't a good idea to be thinking of Project Maestro, especially when there could be government Adepts snooping around. A brief sensation of the world spinning came over her; but she managed to stabilize herself. She was feeling a lot stronger after she had gotten some food and peaceful rest. Miranda cautioned her to continue eating carefully and to avoid transitioning from rural to urban air often – apparently less polluted air could aggravate the toxins in her lungs.

Despite feeling better, Aria knew that she wasn't going to be able to run for very long. Her body was getting more aches; the doctors in Night City had only been able to do so much for her enhanced body. Her natural flexibility had helped her quite a bit – but even so, her muscles were tightening dangerously over bone. She had seen what happened when people put off their maintenance upgrades too long. She needed maintenance and she needed it badly. She just didn't want to admit it. And there was only one place that she could get it. Survival was more important than her pride.

She took a deep breath, *"Piano, I think we need to go back to Project Maestro."*

Aria knew that her internal voice was shaking, she couldn't help it.

"I had a feeling that you might say that."

"It kills me to even think of it as an option, but it seems like our safest option at this point in time. We don't know much about Fugue, people are going to be coming after us because of the wanted poster...if we go in on our own, maybe things won't be as bad."

Aria looked around, she needed to find somewhere to talk. While her face looked neutral while she was talking to Piano, she couldn't help but be paranoid. She never knew when some mega-corp Adepts were hanging around. The more powerful ones would be able to pry into her mind no matter how much she shielded herself. Thankfully Orpheus Ridge was full of nooks and crannies and she was able to find one quickly.

"You know what I'm going to say, Aria."

She did. He would say that going back to Project Maestro would allow them to get the medicine to eradicate scorched atmosphere lung toxicity from her body. It would allow them to get information on Fugue. It would allow her to get her body evaluated. But she knew there would be punishment – isolation, interrogation. And eventually getting placed back in active rotation. She couldn't imagine working for the government after what she, Light, and Jinto had discovered. It would be more difficult to escape from the facility itself, but Aria did know that Project Maestro had weaknesses. All the Opera knew that.

"Do you think we'll be able to find the medicine on the black market?" Aria asked while leaning against a battered brick wall.

"Probably not. It seems like a type of medication that the government would keep all to themselves, doesn't it? Military access only."

Aria's mouth twisted downward. She knew the government well enough to know that Piano was right. If the medicine was on the black market, people would be replicating it. There would be fewer scorched atmosphere related deaths.

She couldn't sit still with all of this on her mind. She could feel the energy flowing through her body. When she was younger and still a performing dancer she had gotten this way before recitals and other types of performances. Though, she remembered it more as excitement and anticipation rather than nervousness.

"Aria, it would answer our questions about Fugue as well. We can't be positive that Fugue is actually

from Project Maestro. They could just as easily be from Karmic Sense."

"I know, but something doesn't feel right about any of this."

"Well, who says we have to stay there? While I would like you to stay and rest up, they're going to put us back into the rotation for missions. All we need is medical care and answers; once we have those, we leave."

It was rare for Piano to tell Aria to deliberately put herself in danger.

"When we left it was at the end of a mission...we didn't break out of the facility..." her voice was flat. Her mind drifted to what she had bee thinking of moments before. Project Maestro had weaknesses. *"But...they do have weaknesses. I'm just as skilled as I was then..."*

Aria sprang to her feet. The idea of going back didn't seem as bad anymore. She had escaped once, she could do it again. Maybe she'd be able to get Light out again and convince Jinto to come with too.

"Well, we should head to the Underground then. Please plot me the quickest path."

"Right on that."

While Orpheus Ridge had once been the shining gem of the government, especially before the skies had been scarred; that act had sent the city into a constant state of change. Even before the skies were scarred, the changes had been happening. The Underground had been built a few months before the sky had been scorched.

The train ran through most large cities and choice smaller ones. Normally Aria and Piano took the ground train; but their encounters with Fugue agents had shaken Aria. They didn't check ID on the Underground; the only downside was that they had a tendency to run into some pretty sketchy people. Those people were drawn to the technological black market that the Underground housed. Aria was usually welcomed, though it was rare for her to use her actual name. They were always trying to buy her skates and goggles off of her. Sometimes people tried to steal them, but that always ended poorly. She was mainly worried about the powerful Adepts that also came with Underground territory – after all, it had originally been created as a way for Adepts to move around without the government knowing. Now it was a slightly more dangerous form of transportation for normal citizens that was still hidden from the higher-ups in the government. She believed it was because it was a valuable resource to the agents that didn't qualify for military-issue vehicles.

Much like the door to Miranda's home, the entrance to the Underground was hidden to those who didn't know where it was. Aria skated up to the industrial waste container that hid the entrance. No one in their right mind would be near one of the containers, but if a person was desperate for technological goods or no-questions-asked transport they would do almost anything. She tapped in the code and waited for the door to crunch open. It opened to a rusted spiral staircase that led deep down into the ground. There was a high, natural ceiling. The train was humming with electricity and there were clumps of people here and there.

One of the 'guards' started approaching Aria. She rolled her eyes, sometimes the guards gave her trouble for looking too much like she was part of the government. While many of the people revered her government tech, the guards recognized that she might be a threat to the Underground. The guard eyed her up and said, "Who the hell do you think you are? People like you don't belong here."

"I'm someone who needs a ride. Someone you've seen before. I belong here more than most!" she spat the words at the guard's feet.

She glared up at him for a few moments, waiting for him to recognize her. She took great pleasure in watching his tanned face melt from tough to fearful in five seconds flat. The last time she had been in Orpheus Ridge the same guard had tried to deny her entrance and she had been forced to kick in his knee to prove who she was.

"Miss Jessica! I'm sorry; I didn't realize it was you. Go right in," she could hear the terror edging into his voice as he rubbed at his knee.

Aria had used many aliases while using the Underground. Everyone knew they were fake, but they didn't question it. It was one of the things that she actually loved about the Underground. Most things she simply tolerated. She made her way towards the train, knowing that it would be leaving soon. Every once and awhile, a person would stop her and try to buy something off of her. Or they would ask if she had the newest version of the anti-aging pill.

"They've all seen me before. Do they really need to try and get my skates and goggles every single time I'm here?"

"Apparently they don't realize that the goggles are administered to everyone who lives in a government run city. Though yours ARE special..."

"They don't need to know that."

Aria took her seat on the Underground's train. Her stop was one of the very last ones. It was about twenty miles out from Project Maestro, in a small city in the state formerly known as Minnesota. She and Light had been very lucky to stumble on the Underground when they did. If they hadn't, they wouldn't have been able to escape. She exhaled and closed her eyes, trying to keep her nerves from overtaking her. The train moved quite slowly to avoid detection from the wrong people, so the trip was longer than she would like it to be. In three days' time, she would be at Project Maestro.

CHAPTER 10

Aria stretched above her head, her elbow and shoulder joints popping loudly. She hated waking up after an artificial sleep like the one that Piano had forced her into for the three days they were on the Underground. It reminded her that her AI had far more control over her body than she liked to think about. It also made her muscles complain for hours after waking.

"I wish you wouldn't put me in an artificial sleep, Piano."

"What else would you have done for three days? You'd just sit up and worry about going back to Project Maestro, I figured that sleep was the better option."

She rolled her eyes as she stood up. Her body swayed for a second, but she regained her composure. At least she was well-rested now. Aria wasn't expecting a warm welcome at Project Maestro, even if she was turning herself in. She knew that she was going to have some extensive and likely unpleasant medical testing. And that would only be after Stratton finished trying to get information from her. The fact that there was a lot of information to try and pry from her wasn't very comforting. Yes, being well-rested would definitely help make everything a little less unpleasant and make sure she kept her wits about her.

As she made her way off of the train, she body doubled over in a cough. No one noticed or cared. They continued on as if nothing had happened. Then again, she knew that she could grow a second head and none of them would bat an eye. Strange was normal on the Underground. She had always expected people to be afraid of scorched atmosphere lung toxicity, and maybe they were, but they didn't show it. Most people seemed so defeated that the disease would almost be a welcome demise, despite it being a painful way to go. She rested a hand on her diaphragm, it still hurt a bit.

Aria pulled her goggles over her eyes in preparation for seeing the sun for the first time in three days. She knew it would hurt like hell if she didn't. She ascended a similar spiral staircase, this one coated in moss and mildew rather than rust, but equally as flimsy. The entrance to this side of the underground was hidden behind radioactive waste bin that was perpetually empty.

The town was a small one, with a check point, café, a small store, and some housing units. There were the ruins of a larger town surrounding it, abandoned buildings and the like. The government had 'spruced' up the small town to use a housing area. When Aria and Light had first come upon it, they had been horrified. This was the exact opposite of what they had wanted. The plan that they had put together with Jinto had been contingent on them finding a larger city where they could blend in for a bit. But their AIs had felt high level technology underground, so they followed directions and had found their savior. Why they had even come back this far from that mission, she would never know.

Aria bristled and put one hand on the waste bin.

"Something just doesn't feel right...scan for AIs, please."

She furrowed her brows; she couldn't risk the Underground being discovered by the wrong people after they had been so helpful to her. She opted to not move; everywhere else was very exposed. Moving away from the waste bin would draw attention to it.

"I feel two Project Maestro AIs. Opera."

Aria cursed in her mind. She hadn't remembered that pairs of Opera patrolled the city as part of their facility duties.

"Do they already know that we're here?"

"Yes. But I can try and mask our position for a while if you would like."

"No, I think it would be best to get this over with as quickly as possible."

Aria stepped out from behind the bin and walked towards the street. Her breathing was coming in short, ragged gasps; part from the irritants in the air, part from being nervous. If she cooperated hopefully everything would be better. She could see two dark haired figures in military issue fatigues. That had to be them. No one wore fatigues for fun. She watched them stiffen as, without a doubt, their AIs told them that Opus 1 was standing before them waiting to be caught. They started sprinting towards her.

"Are they who I think they are?"

Piano didn't have a chance to answer as the two figures came into sight. Naima and Keiran, Opus 3 and Opus 4, respectively. She had always thought that if they were able to have children, that they would have the most gorgeous kids ever. Keiran was the epitome of tall, dark, and handsome while Naima was an olive skinned spitfire with dark hair and dark eyes. Unfortunately, all Project Maestro operatives were sterilized pretty early on to eliminate the possibility of pregnancy if they ended up in a compromising position. Of the Opera that could have been on duty, these were the last two she would have wanted to find her.

"Opus 1?" Naima said, her voice smooth as glass.

"Indeed."

She understood the need to ask. Aria didn't exactly look like she usually did. She knew the other Opera were used to her looking strong and put together. She knew that she wasn't exuding either of those. Being on a train for three days had a tendency to do that.

Keiran scoffed, "And you've come back on your own? Didn't think I'd live to see *that* day."

Aria was already getting irritated with Keiran; that didn't bode well. They had never gotten along very well. They were just opposites. Stratton had learned very quickly that letting the two of them work together ended up with one of them having a black eye or worse.

"So it seems. Are you going to take me back or do I have to go bang on the door myself?"

"Be careful, Aria. You're in no condition to fight, much less fight two Opera at once. You know Keiran won't hesitate to punch you in the face. Just because you're an excellent fighter..."

"Don't worry, I have no intention of fighting them. I will go with them quietly. You can tell that he already wants to fight me and he'll do anything to get me to throw the first punch. Too bad they're on patrol, eh? I can taunt him all I want."

"That doesn't mean that he can't 'accidentally' hurt you."

Aria felt a pang in her chest. Piano's caring had a strange effect on her.

Keiran and Naima were on either side of Aria as they walked back to the checkpoint. From there, they would be able to call for a vehicle. After even more sarcasm from her, Keiran had punched her across the face. Since then, she could tell that they were too in shock to taunt her about returning to Project Maestro. Jinto had managed to get some messages out to them – no one believed that she was ever coming back. Apparently that had made Stratton want her to come back even more.

Aria decided to break the silence, looking between her two fellow Opera, "Do either of you know what Fugue is?"

She watched as Naima looked over at Keiran, the expression on her face was nervous, "Yes, I know what Fugue is."

"Would you please explain what they are to me? They were hunting me down while I was running. I was shocked that Stratton the bastard didn't send another Opus."

The other girl hesitated again before saying, "They were created to replace the Opus Project. Opus was deemed a failure about six months ago."

Aria's gut churned a little bit. While the original group of Opera had clearly had a few bumps along the road, each of them had become a successful elite assassin. Maybe the new generation of Opera was more stubborn than they had ever been. It was the look on Naima's face that made her more apprehensive. The older girl's face was twisted into defeat and fear. One of the first things they had learned was to hide fear, lest an enemy use it to their advantage.

She couldn't help but blurt out, "What?!"

"Between you and Light abandoning your duties, of which, what the hell were you thinking? Neither of you had any problems with the work we did before that. What the hell happened?" Keiran snapped as he jerked Aria's arm painfully. When no answer came, he continued. "That...and the new generation of Opera fought the training more than any of us ever did. The government demanded that a new specimen be designed."

Aria felt her heart sink towards her feet. She wasn't about to tell Keiran of all people why she and Light had fled. She had known for a long time that the government was corrupt – but it wasn't until she, Light, and Jinto had been on a mission to assassinate someone who had learned some information that they had discovered the true extent of the corruption. Because she and Light hadn't been able to work for a government that was capable of such a foul act, they had left. Jinto had stayed to make everything look less suspicious. And to act as a mole within the Project Maestro facility – he had gotten them some information, but both she and Light understood the difficulty of getting out an encrypted transmission. She sighed. Fugue was just another reminder that she wasn't strong enough to continue through her duties despite what she had learned. A real Opus would have been able to keep working.

"Do you know anything else about Fugue?" Aria said while trying to mask her shock.

"You know, Opus 1, you haven't changed at all," Keiran said with a smirk. "We tell you that the Opus Project was declared a failure and you decide its your fault."

"Would just answer my damn question?"

"*Aria, be careful.*"

"What would I know? I'm just a failed Opus after all. I don't know anything."

Aria glowered at Keiran. She had never liked and him and probably never would. And she was sure it had something to do with the fact that he knew how to make her angry in less than sixty seconds. The only good that had come from the interaction was a little bit of information about Fugue.

CHAPTER 11

Aria leaned her head against the slightly padded wall of the isolation room. She had been in the room pretty much since she had arrived at Project Maestro, which had been several days. She marked the passing of days by the plates of food they brought her. She knew exactly why she was in isolation. The room severed her connection with Piano and left her very off-balance. She had figured out somewhere along the way that it was an Adept trick, but she wasn't sure exactly how it worked. Adepts were weird that way. Either way, whoever was going to be interrogating her (she didn't want to assume that it was Stratton) was going to want her to be off her game. The best way to throw an Opus off was to take away that one thing they had to trust. The one thing that kept them calm.

Her head was throbbing. She had managed to tick off Keiran enough with some off-hand comment that he had beaten her pretty badly. He had made some excuse that the guards on duty had been forced to accept at face value. As far as she could tell, she had cracked a rib or two and would have some nasty bruises the next day. They had confiscated her contacts and stripped the black out of her hair, they had mercifully allowed her hair to remain pink. Project Maestro had accepted long ago that the color she preferred for her hair was pink (even if she would dye it to something natural for many missions). They had also given her standard issue fatigues that they had made them start wearing right after AI implantation. She felt lucky.

She heard the hydraulics hiss as the locks slid out of place and the electronic whine of the door opening. She steeled her nerves and prepared for their worst. Stratton filled the door. Aria resisted the urge to scoff; someone had been taking their anti-aging pills. His face was basically the same as it had been when she had first met him, though his rich brown hair had a few shocks of gray running through it. One might have called him fat, but she knew better. His thickness was from muscle, and a lot of it, at that. Despite her humor a second before, he was an intimidating person and his mere presence made her shrink against the cool, black wall.

"Hello Opus 1. Good to have you back with us. I always knew you would come to your senses."

Aria nodded sharply, she didn't want to dignify Stratton's presence with a verbal response. Her eyes were downcast; she hated being alone with him. Every time she was she couldn't help but feel incredible sadness radiating from him. She futilely reached out to Piano, wishing that she could hold him that very moment.

"You know you can't reach Piano when you are in this room. It rarely affects an Opus as much as it affects you," Stratton paused, his hands clasped behind his back as he sauntered around the room. "I just have a few simple questions for you – I don't want you conspiring with Piano for answers."

She rolled her eyes, not caring if he saw; had she wanted to 'conspire', as he put it, she would have discussed it on the Underground, not during the interrogation. She had figured out pretty early on that Stratton had an uncanny way of knowing when the Opera were speaking with their Ais. It seemed like it would be easy to know – but most of the Opera were able to keep up a conversation with a person and their AI.

"Your preliminary diagnostic scans indicted that you had contracted scorched atmosphere lung toxicity, but that the disease was in stasis. There were also traces that an Adept had used their powers on you recently. You went to that women, didn't you?"

Aria didn't dare answer that. Miranda was a possibly unstable Adept who had escaped Oculus Mentis. The fact made her a huge target for Project Maestro operatives and even some ambitious mega-corporations who weren't afraid of powerful Adepts.

The way Stratton was acting filled her with hate. He was playing the role of concerned parent well, just enough worry in his voice to almost make Aria think he actually cared about her.

There was also just enough displeasure to make her almost feel ashamed for leaving.

A lie of omission seemed to be the perfect way to go about things, "An Adept managed to halt the progress of the disease. The person also mentioned that the disease could fully relapse."

"We have medication for it. You will be receiving a full dose shortly. I really must know who managed to stop the disease; the government could use their help."

Aria resisted the urge to roll her eyes again; he didn't know her reasons for leaving, but even so, he should have been able to figure out that 'helping' the government wouldn't be able to sway her. She wasn't thirteen anymore.

"My sources are classified, as you would expect of any Opus. I pay good money for their silence as well."

And she did pay handsomely for confidentiality. He didn't need to know that Miranda never accepted money.

"You admit that you're an Opus? My, that's strange, I never thought I'd hear you say that again."

She narrowed her eyes, she couldn't read his precise motives. She had been forced to admit that she was an Opus before; but it was no secret that she had never stopped calling herself an Opus. It sounded cooler than saying she was an enhanced human. She breathed out slowly, she could play his game for now, "Can't run away from destiny forever, sir."

It burned her tongue to call him sir. While not disrespectful by nature, she couldn't respect that man in any way, shape, or form. Not after all he had done. Aria was quite aware that he was simply the government's puppet, put in his place because he was good at what he did; good at breaking people and molding them to his will through any means necessary. She didn't care.

"One more question, then we'll get you to the medical wing," as he said this, Aria felt a genuine smile spread across her face. She had never been overly fond of the medical wing; but it implied that she would be away from Stratton. It also meant that she would be back with Piano.

"The medical report mentioned that there are numerous awful scars on your back as well as your breasts. Also, the large scar on your right arm. They're concerning enough that I have to question you about them."

The body of an Opus was a road map of scars. Project Maestro had taken to documenting them in hopes of keeping track of the numerous injuries an Opus sustained in the line of duty. She understood why he was obligated to ask; the scars implied that someone had taken advantage of her. She resisted the urge to smirk, Babylon had given her the scars with his metal claws during the times they had been intimate. This gave her the perfect opportunity to mess with Stratton's mind.

"The scar on my right arm is from an overly skilled mark. I was careless and out of practice because I was on the run at that point. I sewed it up myself, hid in a dumpster because I saw Keiran out on mission. I later had a health professional take a look at it," she paused and ran her fingers along the scar before diving into the story of the rest of the scars. "My over-enthusiastic, devilish friend did it, nothing bad happened. Rather enjoyed it, actually," her voice was purposely innocent and sweet.

She watched his face morph from what appeared to be actual concern to a mask of horror. He seemed frozen and she wondered if she would just be able to walk past him. He shook his head, his whole body shuddering, like he was a dog shedding water from his body. She stared intently as he motioned through a small window to the guards who were standing just outside the door.

The guards entered the room with apprehension. Aria grinned in her mind; their hesitation meant they were still afraid of her. They grabbed her by her upper arm and eased her out of the room. She tensed up and waited for the uncomfortable sensation of Piano returning to her mind. She imagined the AI being forced back into its home was akin to being shot in the face; it caused blitzing pain to splinter across her skull for a split second.

"*Piano?*"

"*I'm here, Aria. They kept you in there for a long time,*" there was a hint of panic in his voice that she rarely heard. "*They were interrogating me. I told them we saw a person to fix your scorched atmosphere lung toxicity, but didn't name names. Its my priority to keep Miranda safe."*

Aria had never really figured out how they were able to question Piano independently. She usually chalked it up to another Adept trick. If they could manage to shield her mind from something that was literally implanted in her nervous system, it wasn't that much of a stretch to interrogate that presence.

"I did the same. I can't let them get to Miranda."

"I see that you're happy to have Piano back with you,"Stratton said while leading her through the winding hallways.

After a few more twists and turns, Stratton dismissed the guards and grabbed Aria's arm to drag her into the medical ward. She hissed in pain as her torso was jarred, her injured ribs crying out. The room had several severe nurses milling about the ten utilitarian beds with the cliched hospital bed hangings. She was ushered over to one of the beds and handed a gown. She felt her face redden, she hated when they did full exams. She glared pointedly at Stratton who still seemed disturbed from before; she smirked as he turned away. As she changed, she heard him snap his fingers.

"What do you want, Stratton? I know most people here bow to your every whim, but this is my jurisdiction," the sharp voice of Marianna Taranis said. "Ah. Opus I."

Aria remembered Dr. Taranis with equal parts amusement and terror. She was a shorter woman with a perfect hourglass figure and curly hair the color of beaten gold. She had stood up to Stratton more times than Aria could count and had won each time.

"Preliminary scans showed scorched atmosphere lung toxicity as well as possible broken ribs."

She watched Taranis pull out a scanning device that had a bright blue light on one end. She waved the device over Aria's lungs and her eyes widened. She then scanned the rib cage and murmured about how many times the bones had been broken. Her cold fingers lingered on the jagged scar that ran along her right arm.

"Sorry to say, Stratton, but the girl is mine for a while. She has scorched atmosphere lung toxicity, bruised ribs, and is malnourished."

Stratton nodded meekly and left, mumbling that Taranis was to get Opus 1 in fighting condition by the end of the week. Aria jumped a little at the sound of laughter and regretted it instantly.

"What did you do to him, Opus 1? He normally has more fight than that."

She told Taranis about how Babylon had given her the scars, but mentioned nothing about Night City, the less the government knew about there being more universes than the one they were in, the better. The woman laughed heartily, "Well, he does view you all as his children. I swear he thinks you lot are all teenagers."

She tensed at the sound of combat boots on the tile floor. She knew it wasn't Stratton, his steps were heavier. No. This was definitely a female. A hand came through the curtains and pushed them out of the way, revealing dirty blonde hair and intelligent blue eyes. The girl's hair fell past her shoulders, though the actual length was hard to determine due to the high ponytail. Light fell across the girl's face, illuminating it to Aria.

She felt her jaw drop, "Madeline? What are you doing here?"

"Opus 10 reporting for duty," Madeline said coldly, her eyes narrowed. She turned her attention to Taranis. "Stratton sent me to keep guard of Opus 1."

"Figures that the oaf would send one of his precious Opera to do his work. Just stay out of my way."

Aria closed her mouth and stared into Madeline's eyes. They were the same size and shape as hers, but a chilling blue instead. She could tell that if she were to stand, they would be almost the same height. Madeline was slightly shorter, and definitely curvier. She assumed that the curves came from being better fed. She couldn't believe that her parents had sent another of their children to Project Maestro after all the letters she had sent. She couldn't believe that she hadn't noticed when her younger sister had started.

"Aria, proceed with caution. It feels like she's going to attack."

She flinched at Piano's tone. It wasn't his normal, quiet tone, but vicious and cold. She took his word though and braced herself. She couldn't let emotion get in the way; today Aria would let herself be Opus 1. Their Opus training had told them that emotion was unneeded, extra baggage. It was something she usually ignored. When she ignored her emotions, she felt soulless, bloodthirsty, and entirely not herself. Stratton considered her a huge success because of that.

"Opus 10, what the hell are you doing here?" Aria knew better than to try using her sister's birth name at this point.

"Project Maestro recruited me when you were seventeen. Pathetic that you didn't notice your own sister in the Opera wing."

Aria wasn't surprised at the venom in her baby sister's voice. Madeline had always been on the sensitive side.

"Why did you come here? You knew what would happen. I sent notice that they were forcing us to be assassins," Aria had hidden the message within the usual drivel about school going well. She had known that at least Madeline would understand it.

"Mum and Dad were proud! They were happy! They *wanted* me to go!" Madeline yelled, her eyes filling with tears.

The words slapped Aria across the face. Her parents were proud and happy. Just as fast as the anger had appeared, it was gone. Madeline was glaring and looking empty. Without a word, she turned on heel and marched out of the medical bay, obviously too angry to care about punishment.

CHAPTER 12

Aria's mind was spinning. Her parents had been proud, they had been happy to send another child to this hell. Something seemed suspicious about her parents pushing their youngest daughter to a military life. She had always imagined they would be outraged at how she was treated.

"Piano, how could they give another of their daughters to Project Maestro?"

No response came, but he buzzed in her mind to calm her down. The fact that he hadn't said anything piqued her interest; it implied that he knew more than he was letting on. She made a note to ask him about that at some point in the future.

"Well, that didn't take long," Taranis said as she clicked into Aria's enclosure. "Small wonder she even showed up for 'duty'. Figures that the oaf would think it's a great intimidation technique to send the younger sister. He should know by now that you're pretty damn unflappable. Maddie on the other hand..." Taranis paused, looking thoughtful. "Sorry, that was unprofessional. Let's get back to your exam."

Aria had been soaking in information and now felt her face twist into a scowl. Still, she allowed herself to be led to an examination room. She went to sit down on the table, but Taranis stopped her.

"I want to take a closer look at those ribs first. Your scorched atmo is halted and bruised ribs are troublesome," Taranis shifted the gown to get a better look at the ribs, whistling low as she, no doubt, got an eyeful of the numerous scars crisscrossing Aria's body. "Alright. I have a new serum that might help this clear up faster. Sit backwards on that chair, dear. I'm going to be fully opening the back of your gown now."

She couldn't help but shiver as a blast of cold, sterile air brushed against her back. Taranis murmured something about staying calm while swabbing her back and side with alcohol. Aria tried to listen to the words, but failed to do so until Piano buzzed in her mind. She exhaled, consciously slowly her heart rate. An Opus wasn't a slave to their fear; they used it as fuel.

"Alright. The serum will be injected into the affected area. Its going to hurt. A lot."

Aria felt a pinch on the right side of her ribcage followed by fire. She let out a strangled gasp as her abdominal muscles gave out, causing her to collapse forward onto the chair. It was unlike anything she had ever felt, like the serum was protectively coating the injured ribs. Gradually, her muscles stopped their spasms and she was able to support herself again.

"The next parts aren't pleasant either, Opus 1 - "

"Please, call me Aria..."

Taranis smiled at her warmly, she seemed pleased, "I've got two sub-dermal spikes for you, Aria. I've tried for years to get them to work properly in other muscles, but they only work well in the trapezius."

The woman muttered on about scientific facts that Aria didn't really care about, but understood to a certain extent. She felt warm hands palpate her upper back, right between her shoulder blades. Taranis stated that she would go on the count of three. She lied; she went on two. Aria howled as the spike settled into the muscle. She hated sub-dermal spikes, she couldn't remember when precisely the government had decided to switch to them from traditional injections, but it had been sometime during her childhood. She didn't believe that they were more effective. Her stream of angry thoughts was broken up by the second spike penetrating the muscle. She bit down on her lips in hopes of not screaming. The coppery taste of blood flooded her mouth. She collapsed forward again, whimpering in pain. She closed her eyes tightly, not allowing the tears to fall, an Opus didn't cry. An Opus didn't acknowledge pain. She swallowed the pain and let it become part of her. Piano buzzed in her mind again; she knew that he wanted to say something, but thought that his words would just get in the way.

"Okay, Aria. Procedures done. I gave you the serum, the medicine for scorched atmosphere lung toxicity, and some broad spectrum antibiotics.

Make sure you eat enough tonight and tomorrow, you need to take better care of yourself," Taranis said while taking Aria's post procedure pulse. She frowned when she saw the bite marks gouged into her lip. "And I'll put a salve on that lip. I wish we still used injections versus the spikes."

"Damn. I'd been hoping this would take longer," she said, furrowing her brows, she didn't want to be in training yet. If they were going to give her more punishment, they would have done so already. Aria did find it weird that Stratton was going easy on them.

"*You never want to be in training,*" Piano said with a laugh. "*Stratton is always harder on you.*"

"Well, I can guarantee you won't be in training tonight; that serum would probably cause more harm than help at this point. You'll be going to upgrades tonight, though," her voice had a hint of regret. "I will tell the oaf to be careful with you. The medicine for scorched atmosphere lung toxicity is rather volatile."

Aria took a small ounce of solace in the fact that she could avoid training for another day. But the fact that training was being traded with upgrades didn't sit well with her either. Upgrades were vital to an Opus. The enhancements made to the musculo-skeletal system were hard on the body to say the least. It was important to keep up with maintenance upgrades, lest their bodies break down under the stress. However, as Aria had discovered, upgrades weren't exactly the most pleasant experiences a person went through.

Taranis left a bit later to let her eat a hot meal. The food sat heavy in her stomach, but she was thankful anyway. While found had been plentiful in Night City, she had never gained back the weight she had lost while running those first six months away from Project Maestro. She found it sad that she weighed less now than she had at sixteen.

"Opus 1? Fancy meeting you here," a familiar male voice said.

"Light?"

"The one and only."

Aria felt guilt cramp in her stomach. He looked awful. There was a large bruise covering the right side of his face and his eye was swollen shut. The bruise was a sickly greenish yellow that told her had received it being brought in or shortly thereafter. His usual smug look was tainted with pain; his reception must have been more violent than hers. Aria wasn't too surprised – Fugue had brought him in. She hadn't asked Stratton about Light because the man might have lied to her to get more information.

"Are you okay? What happened after..."

"Fugue beat the crap out of me. Broke a few ribs, sprained my back, you know, annoying injuries," he paused for a moment to roll his eyes. She thought it was creepy when only one eye moved. "So I spent time in the med ward. Then a few days in isolation, followed by some interrogation. I just joined the roster for active duty a day ago or so. No one is deployed right now. I guess its six month physicals and upgrade time."

Aria was surprised by the lack of punishment again. He seemed to be handling the transition to Project Maestro very well, almost like they had never left. A few minutes later, Light was escorting her towards the upgrade room. He was gripping her arm like Stratton did when he moved her around. The rational part of her mind understood that it was standard operating procedure for a moving potentially hostile person. The irrational part of her wanted to question her snarky friend's motives.

"Good luck, Aria," he said, his voice full of empathy. No Opus liked going to the upgrade room.

She cursed internally, they had reached the door without her noticing. The upgrade team was ready for her in their light blue outfits and masks. They motioned for her to lie down on the surgical steel table, which she did without any disobedience.

"Hello there, girly. Good to see you back. We've got three years of upgrades to catch up on. I'm surprised your muscles didn't fracture your tibias...anyway, you know the drill Opus 1," Eli Freeman said from behind his blue, cloth mask. She had always liked Eli. He was one of the few staff members that let the Opera call him by his first name.

Aria was very familiar with the procedure. They had to put her under so they could work directly with Piano. It was a technique that Eli had pioneered (with the medical assistance of Mariana Taranis). The upgrade team got an IV in her arm quickly and with little pain. She felt the strong sedative start pulsing through her veins. While she slept, Eli would be able to work with Piano directly.

The sedative was potent. A moment later, Aria felt herself tumble into her mind. The upgrade team trapped her in a cage of thoughts, inducing a temporary semi-coma. She would never get used to the feeling of being trapped in her mind. Unlike Piano's clean, white realm, her mind was dark and claustrophobic. It made her want to reach out to him, but it would be futile. The dreaming would start soon.

She opened her eyes. Light and Jinto were flanking her, the three of them were laughing raucously. She remembered that mission; it had been a near failure, but by some fluke Jinto had saved them all. They were young enough to find humor in the situation almost immediately. They were waltzing through the halls of Project Maestro like they owned the place. She was only seventeen years old and already a seasoned killer.

"Did you see the guy's face when I slipped out of his 'secret' passage?" Jinto laughed, his gray eyes closed shut, dark red hair swinging with each breath. "Nothing is secret when its posted on the internet!"

Aria's past-self laughed again, "Good thing you popped out, too. Light and I were toast!"

They were wandering through the halls of the Opera wing aimlessly; they had hours until their briefing with Stratton. She hadn't been surprised in the least when they had found themselves by the cafeteria. Food had been hard to come by on the mission.

"Looks like we've got some new recruits," Light said, a smirk playing on his lips. "Guess we aren't the government's last hope anymore."

Aria looked across the cafeteria to a table of teenagers she didn't recognize. There were six of them; she guessed they ranged from fourteen to seventeen. Four girls and two boys. She made note that they still looked innocent.

"Piano, do they have AIs yet?"

"Some of them, yes. Three of them do. Sforzando, Nocturne, and Crescendo are now in hosts. The Project Maestro database tells me the other three receive AIs tomorrow. Teams haven't been chosen yet."

She smiled, or at least her mouth twitched upward. It always amused her when Piano tapped into the Project Maestro database; it was something that Opera weren't supposed to have complete access to. It had only taken the original seven Opera a few days to figure out how to gain access to most of the information.

Aria walked toward their table, yelling to Jinto to grab her some food. He would be more likely to listen than Light. She wanted to meet the people she could possibly work with in the future. She stopped in front of the table, her bandaged right hand resting on her hip. Closest to her was a girl with tanned skin, dark brown hair, and deep green eyes; her face was surprised. Next to her was another girl, this one with silvery blonde hair and gold-hazel eyes. One of the males sat next to her, his hair was light brown and curly, his eyes were gray. Then there was a girl with dirty blonde hair fierce blue eyes. The second male was on her right, honey blonde hair nearly covered his brown/red eyes. And finally there was a girl with light auburn hair and brown eyes.

"Hi, I'm Opus 1, pleasure to meet you all. I just wanted to welcome you all to the facility on behalf of my team. Opus 2 and Opus 6 are my teammates. I look forward to the possibility of working with you. If you guys have any questions, feel free to ask any of us, provided we aren't on a mission. See you around!"

Aria flounced back to Jinto and Light. She was sure the recruits had been welcomed by the staff, by various guards, but they were the first team back from mission. One of the Opera teams had to welcome them, might as well have been her.

"Just like you to welcome new recruits," Jinto said, his voice full of warmth and fondness. "Light would have scared the poor kids."

The three started laughing, but the sound was fading. She was pulling out of the dream. She knew she was in the upgrade room, but couldn't focus on anything.

"Opus 1 - "

She heard Eli's voice, but it was fuzzy, like her ears were stuffed with cotton balls.

"Opus 1, girly, how are you feeling?"

Aria squinted her eyes shut and said, "Very disoriented. I'm very sure that when I stand up I will require assistance." She had managed to sound relatively collected, but her voice wavered more than she would have liked.

The dream settled into the forefront of her thoughts. Horror flew through her mind; she hadn't recognized her baby sister in the dreamed memory. The girl with dirty blonde hair and fierce blue eyes. Madeline had been a new recruit and Aria had been the one to greet them – and she hadn't shown any signs of recognition.

"Piano...are you there?"

His voice did not come immediately like it usually did. Her mind felt strangely empty, which put her more on edge.

"And I can't reach Piano yet. What did you do?" There was a hint of threat in her voice.

Another team member helped Aria sit up slowly, supporting her upper and lower back. Upon being vertical, her world turned upside down and a strong wave of nausea came over her. She leaned over the side of the table, vomited, and groaned.

Eli's face was concerned, but he took the time to gather his thoughts; she knew that he had dealt with upset Opera more than he cared to admit, "The upgrades we gave you shouldn't be causing vertigo. The one that allows Piano to better monitor your health can cause mild dizziness. I've never seen I this bad. The next one was to help with your blood sugar problems, to help the connection between you and Piano. Then we gave you the usual ones for bone, muscle, and the immune system. I'm confused on why you feel *so* bad."

"*Ugh, Aria, I'm here now...I feel awful.*"

"Piano says he feels awful as well."

"Its not too surprising," one of the other team members said; she watched him shrink as Eli glared at him. "You were the first Opus. We've always had issues with your upgrades." She could tell that he had carefully omitted some choice information.

"*I dreamed about Madeline...*"

"*Not necessarily bad.*"

"*I'm a horrible sister. I didn't even recognize her.*"

The upgrade team was slowly bringing Aria to a standing position. The floor felt slanted to her; she was grasping the arms of two men very tightly. She knew the disorientation would pass in time, but it was still a concern. The team was right, her upgrades had always been rough, but they had never been this bad before.

CHAPTER 13

It took Aria nearly three hours to fully recover from the upgrades and even after that amount of time, she still felt a little dizzier than normal when she stood up. But in general, she felt fine – the upgrade team had assured her that she would feel better after some sleep. As awful as an Opera felt after upgrades, they always bounced back fast, faster than most people anticipated. Sure, they still might have some aches and pains from the serums taking hold in their body; but they were more than capable of continuing their regular duties. Now she and Piano were waiting for an escort. She wouldn't be allowed free-reign of the building until she had spoken with Stratton the next day. Being allowed free-reign confused her. She had left her duties – being given free-reign of the Opera wing wasn't a punishment. Aria had anticipated punishment.

"Piano, Eli gave one of the other team members a rather severe look when he was commenting on how my upgrades have been rough because I was the first Opus. This is common knowledge. I'm just wondering why Eli, who is normally laid back gave a death glare that rivals the one Taranis has."

"I never told you how it was that first week."

Aria felt her pulse quicken; she remembered their first week together. She had woken up after the procedure and they had plugged in to help the bond form. They had gone to classes and learned so much together.

She could feel how conflicted Piano was before he even started speaking, *"There were some issues with your implantation procedure. I was ordered to never tell you. I figured it wold come up some day, though. You Opera are too smart and observant for your own good,"* he paused, his voice sounded heavy and melancholic. *"Before I was implanted in you, I learned many things. There were some initial experiments with AIs being implanted in humans. They all failed. You were the first **real** experiment. They had theorized that an AI would take immediately. They were wrong, it takes a few minutes,"* another pause, Aria was shocked when it sounded like he was crying. *"They gave you an extremely high dose of glucose so I would take in your mind easier. It put you into a coma for a week,"* he paused once more, his voice seemed detached as he continued. *"It almost killed you. One week alone in your mind. It was...awful."*

Aria didn't know what to say. She would never have guessed, but now that the information was processing, it made sense. It explained her erratic blood sugar levels. They must have taken excellent care of her muscles and nutrition while she was comatose, because there had been no atrophy and she had been about the same weight.

"I'm sorry I kept this from you, Aria. It killed me to hide it, but it was a direct order from Stratton to not tell you anything regarding our implantation or the experiments."

"Its...alright. I understand."

A harsh knock pulled Aria from her reverie. Apparently her recovery was done. She pushed off the soft bed and stood up slowly. Her normally long strides were more of a shuffle. She reached the door and punched the open button, hoping that her escort would be someone nice, like Jinto or Light. The door whirred open and she was staring up at Keiran's fiercest scowl.

"God, you look awful."

"No one looks good after upgrades," she said, her voice snippy.

"Come on, Opus 1, lets make this easy on both of us," Keiran said as he grabbed her upper arm. He sighed in what she figured was irritation. "They told me that you may require assistance with walking, is this true?"

Aria bristled at the mention of assistance, "No, I should be fine. The disorientation has mainly cleared up."

With that, they were walking through the winding hallways of the Project Maestro complex. She wasn't entirely surprised that Keiran was her escort, he and Cadenza preferred working the night shift. Jinto and Light were usually swing shift, like she had been back in the day. Her thoughts were interrupted as they breezed past the

Opera wing. Aria felt her stomach clench, that didn't bode well.

Before she let herself jump to conclusions, Aria said, "Did they move my room? It's late and I've had a rough day."

That was the closest she had ever been to admitting weakness to another Opus, excluding Jinto and Light.

"Stratton wants to see you before you sleep."

She closed her eyes for a moment. She didn't want to deal with Stratton tonight. Being in the medical ward and having upgrades in the same day had made her irritable and slightly paranoid. This would not go well.

"He really wants to make me suffer, doesn't he?"

"I'm sure he just wants to make sure you're doing better than you were when you came in."

Despite Piano's warm buzz in her mind, Aria did not feel comforted.

Keiran shoved her towards Stratton's door and sneered when she tumbled to the ground. Her wrists ached for a moment as she pushed herself to her knees and stood up. She glared at Keiran and knocked on the door.

She heard a gruff 'enter' and opened the door. Unlike most of the Project Maestro facility, Stratton's door was wooden. Pretty much anything built after the skies were scorched was electronic. Having a wooden door just showed Stratton's age even more in Aria's mind. Her eyes flickered over Stratton, the shadows of his office highlighted what the aging pills had not been able to smooth out. The shocks of gray that ran through his dirt brown hair were even easier to see in this light. She thought she saw concern register on his face for a split second, but then he seemed to smile at her haggard appearance. She knew that the next day would be hell.

"Please, do sit down, Opus 1," he said, motioning to the chair across from his messy desk.

Aria tensed, it was almost like he was treating her like an equal. This seemed odd to her, he always treated them like soldiers and he the drill sergeant. On a good day, they were naughty children and he the angry parent. Still, she sat down warily, bringing her narrowed eyes to his.

"I know your intentions for returning are not pure. I know you have not realized how important the work you were doing was, but I don't care. I know you have questions and I have some for you," Stratton said while twirling a pencil around his finger.

"Be careful, Aria. You know he's tricky."

"Noted."

While she knew that Stratton was merely the puppet, he was highly intelligent. The government had wanted the person who ran Project Maestro to have an intellect as high as the genius children he was working with. While the teenagers were all book-smart, Stratton was a tried and true military genius; he could break people easily and made iron-clad strategies. Stratton was a force to be reckoned with.

She knew that being straightforward would be the best plan at this point in time. She said, "I came back because of the obvious health issues I was having and dire need for upgrades. I also came back to ask about Fugue. They were hunting me for weeks before the symptoms of scorched atmo became problematic. They did serious damage to both of us, which isn't entirely out of the ordinary, but I don't think you gave the order to harm us that badly. You would say to bring us back, but never injure the bio cord."

"As I'm sure you know, Fugue is Project Maestro's new experiment. While Opera work in teams, the work you do is still basically as an individual. Fugue functions as one. Because of this, they are considered more useful than an Opus," Stratton paused for a moment while reaching for a glass full of amber liquid. "I'm sure you've heard that Opus has been declared a failure."

Aria nodded slowly. The smell of alcohol wafted from the glass in his hand. Though from what she had gathered Fugue operated just like Opera.

"Another supposed plus of the Fugue program was that they were supposed to be flawlessly obedient."

The word 'supposed to' caught Aria's attention, but she was tired enough not to question it at this point in time. Stratton was a very 'need-to-know-basis' sort of person and she wasn't in the 'need' area at the moment. She could feel that he wanted to say more, but didn't push it. She watched him take another sip from his small glass.

"I want to know why you ran, Opus 1."

Aria choked on her breath. She knew that she would have to answer that at some point, but she had hoped she would be better rested and in a better frame of mind.

"*You knew he would ask. Lies of omission work best with him. Tried and true.*"

Piano was right. Panicking wouldn't help anything.

"Light and I discovered some information that we shouldn't have. We were no longer comfortable performing our duties."

Stratton smiled lazily, the amusement that played across his features didn't sit well with her, "And what of Jean Thomas, Opus 2?"

Aria took a deep breath as she held Stratton's blue gaze, "Jinto went back and reported that we had been separated during the mission, which is technically true. He continued working to keep us safe." Jinto had reported to her that he had the distinct feeling that Stratton knew he was just trying to keep she and Light safe.

That was a little more honest than she had intended to be, but there was no undo button in real life.

"It must have been quite the bit of information for both you and Light to leave."

She raised her eyebrow at him, she didn't know if he had honestly intended for that bait to work.

Maybe that would have worked when she was thirteen, not when she was twenty-three.

Stratton rolled his eyes and finished off his small glass of alcohol, "I need your help."

Aria felt her face go slack. She couldn't remember a time that Stratton had seriously wanted her help. If he needed help, he ordered them to do it. This was distinctly *not* an order.

"Be careful. Him needing your help can only be bad."

"I know. There's going to be some serious strings attached to this."

He looked pained for a moment, his fingers wrapped tightly around his empty glass, "There are two Opera who have recently escaped, Opus 9 and 12. I don't particularly care *why* they ran away. It's that they're in grave danger. Our Adepts have been tracking them, but as of yet, we haven't sent anyone to retrieve them."

"And why does this matter to me?" Aria said, playing the not-caring card might get more information out of Stratton, especially since he had been drinking.

"Because as you've experienced, Fugue targets rogue Opera. Its something that I have little to no control over. Fugue is chasing after two girls who are running because they want to have a life together. They aren't focusing on the threats that are chasing after them. Ava and Katya need your help, Opus 1. They will die if you do not help them."

CHAPTER 14

Aria was lying in her old bed in her old room, Project Maestro had kept it for her on the odd chance she would come back. Perhaps they had known she would come back all along, just like Stratton knew that Aria would never fully be his. It was cleaner than as she left it – she assumed that they were covering their tracks. Stratton had given her some time to think it over, especially since he had ordered that Fugue be pulled back in. She was to have a decision by sundown the next day. She sighed, it was stereotypical for it to be sundown. But she understood why he was having her decide by then. Aria would be deployed around 4am if she accepted this, which meant an early dinner and lights out for her. The fact that Stratton had appeared to give her a choice was interesting – it didn't feel like something General Crawford would allow.

She had been dismissed shortly after he had said the girls would die if she didn't help them. She had been unable to say anything really intelligent – she had been too caught off guard by him saying the girls' names. General Crawford had been pretty strict about the staff sticking with their code names rather than their given names.

"Do you think he's actually going to give us a choice, Piano? Giving choices isn't exactly his style."

"No, in the end, if you decide to not go through with this, he will find a way to make you do it for him. And it will be a hell of a lot more unpleasant if he does it that way. He's not accustomed to hearing 'no'."

"Even if he's going to make us do this, I don't know how I feel about it. I don't want them to die. But...it would be hypocritical for me to bring them in when I left myself. But Fugue...they injured Light's bio cord."

The connection on the back of an Opera's neck was almost like their lifeline. It was cruel to injure it and could kill them if something bad happened to it as it was an extension of the spinal cord. Light had been lucky to live through the ordeal. Plugging in was the only way that an Opus really dealt with the disembodied voice in their head. It gave them a face to match the voice.

Aria sighed. It was already close to wake up. Soon enough, it was morning, and while Aria hadn't slept, she still felt quite revitalized. Lying down without being poked or prodded with needles and spikes had done enough for her body. She heard the wake up alarm clang in the hallway and she stood up and slowly got dressed. Aria knew that she would have no leeway. She put on the standard issue fatigues that were stashed in her closet and grimaced at their looseness. She preferred tight clothing with good mobility, loose clothing just made her look thinner. She figured that her years of dance had made her fond of tights and leggings. She slipped into her combat boots and laced them up tightly. She ran her finger forlornly against the side of the boot, hoping that they would contain her roller blades. She knew they would not, Stratton had confiscated her goggles and boots upon her arrival.

Within a few minutes, her comfort and thoughts were interrupted by a loud knock on the door that told her it was time for breakfast. She reported to the door, shoulders back, looking like an entirely different person. When Stratton opened the door, he seemed pleasantly surprised to see her ready to go. When she entered the hallway, she could see all the other Opera lined up on their doors. She made eye contact with Jinto who was stretching languidly in his door frame, his long red hair pulled back into a neat ponytail. She thought it was strange to see original Opera mixed in with all the new ones. She did take note of the two empty doors and felt her stomach constrict painfully.

They went through the motions of breakfast, which delighted Aria to no end, especially as she was seated with her three-man cell. Food was a precious commodity to her. Aria felt guilty for devouring the ample breakfast placed before her – she knew that there were people out there starving. The food was perfectly balanced for the mind and body of an Opus – 2,000 calories per meal. It seemed excessive at first, but it was merely so the Opera could maintain weight and mental capacity. She was surprised that her stomach didn't become upset at the amount of food she ingested – since she had left Night City she hadn't been eating near enough.

After breakfast, they made their way to the training center. Even though they were all very well trained, especially the original seven Opera, maintenance training was necessary. It was an integral part of the six month checkup. They would learn new techniques and have their overall fitness assessed. With the amount of genetic work that had been done of their musculature, it was key for the Opera to be checked up on every few months.

Stratton started barking out orders to all the Opera, pairing the ones who had not yet been evaluated up for sparring, telling the ones who had been evaluated to power lift, She noticed that he was purposely splitting up the mission groups. Then he turned his gaze to Aria.

"Opus 1, you're with me today."

His words were not a request. Aria made her way over to Stratton, hiding her fear as well as possible. She settled her face into a scowl. The logical part of her mind (and Piano) told her that Stratton was pairing up with her because he wanted to evaluate her. The irrational portion of her mind knew that it was a scare tactic. He wanted to break her. She sighed, it was probably a little from both options. They went through some basic warm up exercises; Aria went through some of her old dance moves and then some stretches. While she did her wide straddle stretch, she felt a sharp stabbing pain in her upper back, near her spine.

Stratton watched as she clutched a hand to her spine, "Opus 1, Taranis informed me that the subdermal spikes will continue to hurt for a little bit. It is normal, you'll be fine."

"*Piano, this is cruel...*"

"*Keep strong. You know what he's doing.*" Aria noted the venom in his voice, but ignored it.

Once she was done stretching, she and Stratton started free-sparring. It didn't take long for the match to evolve into an anything goes brawl. Aria had Stratton purely on the defensive, showing him how very far she had come. When they had first started learning how to fight, she had refused to strike her opponent and had barely tapped them with her hands and feet. Even before she had started doing assassinations for Project Maestro, her outlook had changed. Kill or be killed. But she had still held back in sparring matches. Stratton had seen the potential and raw talent because of her dance skills. Now she was aggressively backing Stratton into a corner.

"I'm impressed," Stratton gasped out as a particularly strong punch sneaked under his guard. "Being on your own made you realize your potential."

Aria threw a beautiful spinning kick that had her body fully horizontal, knocking Stratton to the ground with ease. She stood over him, her scowl etched further into her face, "No. It made me realize how foolish I was."

Stratton did a rapid spinning sweep, making Aria tumble to the ground. She was on her feet almost as fast as she had fallen – but it had allowed him to gain a fighting advantage. She blocked all of his attacks, but knew that she would lose the match if she continued blocking. Each time she tried to counter, he blocked it without any effort. She knew that all the other matches had stopped, everyone was watching the match intently.

Strange things happened when Opera started fighting seriously, or even sparring. The consciousness of the AI and the host blended together, allowing their reflexes to increase almost exponentially. The AI and the host were equally in control in times of stress – if the host didn't see the punch coming, likely the AI did.

Aria felt Piano meld into her limbs, into her breathing. The strikes that Stratton was throwing were fast and varied, but now she knew that she could stop them. She caught his leg and went to sweep him, but felt his long limb slip from her grip. She ducked the kick that flew towards her head, thankful that Piano had caught that hint of motion. She watched his face switch from amused amazement to serious in a split second. His entire posture shifted and then she felt a swift punch to her diaphragm breech her guard and force the air from her lungs and caused her to tumble to the ground. Aria writhed on the ground for a moment, her eyes snapped shut and her mouth moving soundlessly and wordlessly, gasping for breath. Stratton sat heavily on her gut, the blade of his forearm across his throat.

"You might be a talented fighter, one of the best that Project Maestro has ever produced. But I'm the one who taught you," he paused to catch his breath. "I can make life hell if you do not save those girls."

Aria glared up at him. She knew that she had lost the match, but she wasn't entirely sure *how* she had lost the match. Stratton might have taught her, but he was a normal human. Having an AI should have given her the advantage. She slipped her hands under his forearm, trying to push him off, even though she knew it was futile.

"Aria, you know you need to give up. Its either relent and say yes, or he's going to blood choke you."

She didn't want to listen to Piano, but she knew that she had to, "I'll do it." The words tasted bitter in her mouth.

CHAPTER 15

"*I don't like this,*" Aria said in her mind, her brow furrowed deeply.

"*I know you don't, but its the right thing to do,*" Piano said. She knew that he had purposely left out the fact that they hadn't had a choice in the matter.

She looked around quietly; she was outside of the Project Maestro complex. The facility was built into several of the bluffs in what used to be known as southeastern Minnesota. From the road side, all a person could see was the bluffs, jagged and steep. On the other side there was a chain of buildings carved into the stone. She had heard rumors of an underground tunnel that burrowed from Project Maestro all the way to Oculus Mentis which was in the isolated north of Minnesota. The area surrounding Project Maestro wasn't as scorched as other parts of the former United States. In most places, the plants were withered and dead, if they even grew. Outside of the facility there were delicate purple and white flowers rising from the ground like smoke.

Sighing, Aria pulled herself back into her mission. Stratton's orders were very clear; locate the girls and bring them back to Maestro. Fight

Fugue if necessary. She didn't really understand why Stratton was having her bring the girls back – if the Opus project had been declared a failure it didn't make sense to bring back the all the rogue Opera. It didn't seem like something that General Crawford would order.

It didn't sit well in her stomach that he couldn't control Fugue's urge to track and bring in rogue Opera. Stratton's description of Fugue being useless didn't sit well with her either. Aria had seen them in action. They were far from useless. Something just wasn't adding up the way it should. She couldn't figure it out now, but she would.

At least she had received new gear out of this. They had revamped her goggles, given them a few new features, and at her request they had kept them blue. She also had new boots that converted into electronic roller blades. She loved them.

Stratton had given Aria very specific information on the girls' last location. The government Adepts had been tracking them since they had left the facility. She was grateful that they had been stupid enough to travel together. Even if they were running to start a life together they should have separated for a bit to make it harder to track them. Its what she would have done if she had been in their shoes. Guaranteed, she and Light had traveled together for a very short time; but no more than three days. These girls had been traveling together for about two weeks. That, combined with the fact that they had stayed relatively close to the Project Maestro base (they had stayed within twenty miles), made Aria think that the girls were foolish.

Aria felt lucky that they had given her clothing back; she had felt alien in the fatigues. She had made a strong argument about blending into the crowds and that military-issue clothing would draw unneeded attention. Her Project Maestro ID would be enough to scare of the more persistent guards. Stratton and some of the other Opera had agreed with her. She smiled at the tightness of her legging-like pants and tank top and the looseness of her trench coat. But there was that sour taste in her mouth and a heaviness in her heart; she was working for Project Maestro again, which was something she had vowed to never do again. Her stomach twisted, but this wasn't helping the government. This was helping two girls who were trying to escape. She could do this, even if it tore her up inside. So long as she wasn't directly helping the government she could justify it. That and Stratton would probably kill Light, Jinto, or Madeline should she try to run off while she was on mission.

Her mind drifted into memories. A fifteen year old her, still in training, screaming at Stratton about not wanting to kill people for a corrupt government. He had literally thrown her into the isolation room. She remembered a pained look on his face; somewhere between regret, horror, and nausea. He had never really gotten physically violent with any of the Opera, Aria suspected that the higher-ups had ordered him not to, but there had always been special occasions. General Crawford was usually around for these moments – they had seemed to amuse the twisted old man.

She poked at the earbud in her left ear. Stratton had insisted that she take it with her just in case she needed help as she wasn't going on mission with her team. Aria hated it; the earbud made her think that Stratton and his lackeys were listening in on her every thought. She hated that she wasn't working with her team. Jinto and Light had always been good company. The worst part about the earbud was that if she took it out, they would assume that she was renegade again and would send Fugue after her. And probably hurt her friends and family. This didn't sit well with her or Piano.

"*What direction are they, Piano?*"

"*They went south. That was foolish of them, there's not much in that area.*"

Aria smiled for a moment, she loved when Piano threw insults, he was usually too polite to do so, then said, "*Remember, they're about my age. Am I foolish?*"

"*You know that you aren't foolish. You knew the risks of leaving Project Maestro. You knew that it could mean your death. You knew that Jinto would only be able to hold up the lie for so long. And more importantly, you knew that they would chase you. These girls are being rash. I understand **why** they're running, but they're leaving a big enough trail that an untrained child could follow them!*"

Aria was aware of the point that Piano had. She, Jinto, and Light had planned meticulously once they had discovered the information; except, of course, the details that couldn't be foreseen until they were on the run. Piano, Andante, and Allegro had overseen everything and made sure their plan was sound, especially because their plan was being made on the fly. She was sure that the girls had consulted with their AIs before leaving, but the plan was full of holes. An AI could see the flaws in a plan because of the information at their disposal. She could only reason that the girls had ignored their AIs' counsel and decided to do whatever the hell they wanted to do.

"Do you know if there are any towns within this area? I know there's the Underground, but we're going to avoid that this time. But I'd almost put money on those girls being in a smaller city."

"Aria, I think you're overestimating their foresight. You know to hide in smaller cities. They'll probably be in some small, broke-down town. Probably still in the standard issue fatigues," Piano said, the bitterness apparent in his voice. He made a sound similar to a person clearing their throat and said, *"But to answer the question, there is a small town about twenty miles out. Go figure."*

"Set our destination as that city and give me some directions, please. Let's test out these new skates!"

Aria reached down to the side of the boots to bring the wheels out and pulled her goggles down over her eyes to project them. The new wheels felt funny to her, larger, but the knew that they would

117

be more stable for skating on rough terrain. She had been shocked when Stratton had handed her new gear; he had looked at her battered gear upon returning to Project Maestro and decided that upgrades were in order. It was one of the nicer things he had done for her. The larger wheels changed her center of balance a little bit, it would take her awhile to get used to fully get used to them. She pushed off with her left foot and felt the wheels start spinning faster than her old skates ever had. These skates were going to be really fast once she was used to them.

"*We're coming up on a road, stick to that for five miles,*" Piano said.

"*Affirmative.*"

It didn't take long for them to get close to the town. The abrupt change from rural to urban air made her lungs ache – Taranis had warned her that she would experience pain and possibly coughing for a few more weeks. She stopped skating fro a moment and leaned against a tree so dead that it creaked. Her shoulders slumped; she missed dancing. She probably missed dancing more than she missed her parents. Aria had been on the fast track to be the prima ballerina at a New York performing arts school; dancing had been her life up until age thirteen. Her audition had been the day before the 'nation-wide youth intelligence testing'.

The day after she had received her acceptance to the school of the arts, the Project Maestro representatives had shown up and talked to her and her parents about furthering her education in a way that would be best for Aria. Education had always been the main priority in her family, so the Project Maestro 'school' had been the apparent best choice to her parents. Everything had started out wonderfully. Aria had been in a class with six other highly gifted teenagers. They were all learning college-level material and beyond. They had even allowed Aria to continue dancing at first. Then the experiments had started.

She stopped leaning on the tree and twirled her way back to the street. She knew that Stratton loved the fact that she was a dancer. She already had the flexibility that the other Opera lacked and had easily learned all the martial arts they were required to learn. She knew that if there were still martial arts schools that she would hold at least one black belt. Opus 1, the first experiment. Their biggest success and failure all in one.

"Aria, take a left at the fork that's coming up. That should bring us to a more industrialized area, at least. Miranda and Taranis warned me that switching between industrial and rural areas a lot could aggravate your lungs."

While the air in rural areas still had the contaminants of whatever had scorched the sky – it was clean from everything else. It was the switching between clean and dirty air that would irritate her newly healed lungs. They just couldn't handle the switch. Not yet at least.

"Noted. Are we coming up on a check point and city or just an industrial area?"

"*Just an area. Aria, are you alright? I'm tracking your thoughts...you seem troubled.*"

Aria scowled a little. As much as she couldn't live without Piano, it annoyed her that he could get so deep into her thoughts without her even realizing it. She felt him buzz around in her mind and couldn't help but smile.

"*I'm alright, Piano. Just...frustrated. It makes me feel conflicted that we're working Project Maestro again. I mean...how could I even **think** of working for them again after...*" she trailed off as her stomach lurched. "*I sometimes wonder that...maybe should have just been a dancer. But then I would never have received you. I can't even imagine what I'd be without you.*"

"*I understand. I often wonder what would have happened if I had been placed in someone else. I wouldn't – couldn't – change who I'm with, though,*" he said, though Aria got the distinct feeling that he was leaving something out.

Aria started skating again, faster than she had ever been able to before. An industrial area began to surround them; smokestacks were spewing black smoke, making the sky look brown rather than orange.

"*These girls definitely didn't pick a good area to go through...*" Piano whispered.

Strangely enough, the smoggy air that permeated through the area didn't hurt Aria's lungs as much as she thought it would. Sighing, she continued skating; at least she knew it would be a quick trip to whatever the city was called.

"Where are we headed?"

"Small town people started calling Southern Industrial Outpost after the attacks. People are so clever," he said, a level of snark that usually only Light used creeping into his voice. *"No internet sources, one or two computers, with limited habitation. There is also a 'general store'."*

Aria frowned a little, the lack of habitation didn't seem like a move an Opus would make. Then again, their entire plan was full of mistakes that, in general, an Opus wouldn't make. She didn't even go to cities as small as Southern Industrial Outpost; she preferred to have a place with an internet source, it made things easier on Piano. She also liked having a decent amount of places to hide. The Outpost wouldn't have much in that means. She was almost positive that the girls' AIs would have cautioned the girls against coming to this place, but it seemed like they were disregarding their AIs; Aria wondered how they could do that. She didn't always listen to Piano, but his words always played into her decisions.

CHAPTER 16

Within the next hour, Aria skated into the small town. The town made her spine crawl uncomfortably, it looked more like a ghost town than a proper outpost. There was a small restaurant, the general store that Piano mentioned, and a few battered housing facilities. There weren't any signs of government influence in the area, at least the girls had been smart in that means.

"*Well, let's run some scans, Piano.*"

"*Scans show vague signs of AIs, a several life forms, likely people, and two computers.*"

"*Noted. Can you identify the AIs?*"

"*Nocturne and Agitato.*"

She remembered laughing years earlier when she found out that Project Maestro had implanted Agitato into a host. She still thought it was a ridiculous decision; a host that matched up with that particular AI was going to have issues with the militaristic views that an Opus dealt with on a daily basis. She sometimes wondered if she was more intelligent than the whole of Project Maestro.

She grumbled a little and continued moving through the antiquated town. An abrupt noise that was similar to a footfall made the small hairs on the back of her neck stand on end. She looked behind her, there was nothing. Frowning deeply, she continued her progress through the town.

"Are there any AIs following us?"

Aria was aware that AIs could feel when they were being tracked and would oftentimes shield themselves. Piano was skilled at tracking without being noticed, just as he was skilled at hiding himself.

"Not that I can feel. Proceed with caution."

She scowled a little, but continued along the directions that Piano was whispering in her mind. His voice led her into a rusting warehouse that had clearly been broken into before. Fugue knew her preference for hiding in warehouses. That fact put Aria further on edge, causing her to go into a low crouch and bring out her small energy knife. Her back was pressed against the wall as she peered around the corner. Again, a sound so similar to footfall brought anxiety straight to the forefront of her mind.

She took a deep breath and saw two filthy young women leaning against the wall. She recoiled, those two girls couldn't be the Opera she had been sent to retrieve. It looked like they had done nothing to defend themselves. She rushed into the room; she could barely feel the life in the girls.

"Aria, NO!"

Piano stopped her mid-stride and made her look into the room with a more analytical eye. She noticed that the two girls were bound together and were completely unconscious. She didn't know how she had managed to miss that at first glance. She was moving too fast.

"A trap."

"*Definitely,*" Piano whispered. "*Scanning for AIs and lifeforms.*"

Aria knew that he wouldn't pick up on anything other than the two girls, whoever had done this knew a few things about her personality, knew it well enough to realize that she'd be paranoid. They would be well hidden. They must have also realized that she'd try to figure out what was going on. She closed her eyes tightly, she needed to think of something to do, anything.

"*I can't pick up anything, but it seems you were anticipating that. Just be careful.*"

"Yes. These people know us better than we think they do."

Aria didn't like this at all, uncertainty made her skin crawl, especially when there were lives other than her own on the line. Still, she knew there was nothing she could really do to figure out the trap. She hated blind missions; they were usually the missions that ended up with her and Light in a very bad position and Jinto bailing them out. But she didn't have her team members to help her this time. She kept her knife out while she silently crept into the room. When nothing jumped out at her, she rushed over to the girls to feel their pulses and make sure their chests continued to rise with each breath.

She heard the footfall again, but this time there were multiple steps. She listened closely; she picked out about six different people. Aria turned around to view the source of the steps and was greeted by six people who she assumed made up Fugue. She picked out Diminuendo quickly and smirked. She stared at the six, Piano provided their names. She assumed that he had been able to pick their names up while they were at Project Maestro. Largo, the tall, bulky male with blonde hair and blue eyes. Elegy, the beautiful woman with long, silvery, blonde hair. Stretto, a man around her height with dark hair and hazel eyes. Grave, a slim woman with brown hair that was cropped extremely short. Rondo, another woman, her hair a rich brown and eyes so gray that they seemed to lack color. Diminuendo rounded them out.

"Six Fugue members for three Opera? Does Stratton doubt your power now?" Aria asked, her voice lashing venom at the six.

"Be care, Aria. They're ready to attack."

She felt Piano begin to meld into her senses as a precaution. Neither of them wanted to be caught off guard with so many opponents. They both knew that a fight was inevitable; Aria could feel it forming in the air.

"Fugue works together. Always," Grave said, her eyes boring into the ground.

"Stratton didn't send us. He was displeased that more Opera escaped and ran away. We will fix the problem," Stretto said, his voice deep and slow.

"Always together, never to part...Fugue will finish what Opus starts..." Diminuendo whispered.

The way they spoke creeped Aria out, there was barely any space between their speech and the intonation matched. They all had the same disdain and utter hatred in their voices. It was like they were one unified mind rather than six separate ones. She shook that feeling away – Project Maestro was horrible, but they weren't that evil. They wouldn't take away someone's personal identity.

Without any telegraph, the six were attacking Aria viciously, putting her on the defensive. She cursed internally, the only weapon she had on her wouldn't equalize the playing field. She was trained in multiple opponent fighting, but had never encountered six well-trained enemies at once. The principle had to be the same; she couldn't let them surround her. She let go of her thoughts, thinking would only get her in trouble at this point.

She gripped the small energy knife in her hand, it wasn't much, but it certainly wouldn't hurt her chances. They fought together, like they were actually a fugue, blending together, yet uniquely separate. As Grave, the slim woman, darted at her, Aria grabbed her arm and threw her neatly into Stretto, Elegy, and Rondo. Before she could really react, Diminuendo had latched onto her back and began to choke her out. How he had gotten behind her, she would never know. Aria gasped for air, knowing that her face was slowly turning purple. She reached up to reflexively stop the choke and the forgotten energy blade stabbed Diminuendo in the arm. He fell from her back, howling in pain. She gazed at the Fugue members on the ground for a moment, she then turned her attention to Largo, the last of Fugue standing. This seemed too easy. They had to be toying with her, but she wasn't in any position to question it at the moment.

"You are strong," he said simply, his ice blue eyes penetrating into her own. "But I am stronger than you."

"Less talk," Aria growled, she hated when opponents pointed out the obvious.

"*Aria, you need to be calm,*" Piano whispered, his voice a distant brush against her mind. "*Don't let him get to you.*"

She dropped back into a fighting stance and motioned for the man to come at her. She had already figured out that he was the strongest of them, his blows had felt like they were cracking bone. But of all the Fugue members, he was the one that had the most telegraph. In the long run, strength wasn't the most important attribute to possess; speed and stamina were the traits that won fights.

He threw several kicks and punches towards her, each painfully telegraphed. Without the support of his five companions, he was nothing.

Aria threw quick snap kicks at him, aiming at his knees, and successfully backed him into the wall. He gasped as she wrapped her left hand around his throat and lifted him off of the ground.

"You will leave me alone, Fugue," Aria said, her arm shaking from the effort of holding up the weight of a full grown man.

"Fugue will never leave Opus alone. We will never leave *you* alone. This isn't the last you've heard of Largo."

"*Aria, let him go. He knows he's defeated. They'll leave us alone for now,*" Piano said. "*It's pretty clear to me that they're toying with us now. Had they wanted to win, they would have.*"

"*I know...*"

Aria dropped Largo to the ground and glared at him. An opponent who knew he was defeated could be more dangerous than an oblivious opponent. They knew they were beaten, they might do something stupid. She kicked him in the gut for some assurance that he wouldn't attack her when she grabbed the girls. She lifted them and left the warehouse without another word.

Once she felt that they were a safe distance away from the building, Aria placed Ava and Katya on the ground outside, and stared down at them. They had both decided to wake up and start flailing around when she was carrying them. After one of them had kicked her head, what little of her good humor had still be there had vanished. The two girls, filthy as they were, were beautiful. One was tan, with deep green eyes and dark brown hair, the other was pale, with silver blonde hair and intelligent gold-hazel eyes. She recognized them, she would put them around twenty-one years old. They looked terrified and showed no signs of recognizing her.

"Relax, I'm not going to hurt you," Aria said, holding her hands up to show that she wasn't armed. She had lost her knife when she accidentally stabbed Diminuendo. "Though I will admit that I do not appreciate being kicked in the head."

"Who are you?" the dark one asked, her voice shaking almost imperceptibly.

"Opus 1. You can call me Aria. I know that you're Opus 9 and 12, names Katya and Ava. I've met you before, but I'm sorry to admit that I can't remember who is who."

"I'm Katya," the dark one said, bringing her eyes up to Aria's.

Aria nodded stiffly. She needed to get the girls back to Project Maestro – then Stratton could rip them apart all he wanted.

"Their blood pressure is through the roof. We need to get them calm before we move. I imagine this is quite stressful for both of them," Piano said, he paused for a second. *"I'll try to reason with their AIs."*

"I can practically feel their fear. I feel horrible bringing them back...but they would have died. I know that."

Aria motioned for the girls to follow her, which they didn't without complaint. They had just watched her take down six people at once.

They didn't have to know that the battle had been strangely easy. She led them into the small cafe that was in the broken town. Aria's wanted posters were plastered all over the walls, the same blank stare looking back at her. She sat down at a booth, the two girls followed. Aria smiled broadly and told them to get whatever they wanted. They both stared at her, asking if she was sure, to which Aria nodded.

"Are you going to take us back to Project Maestro?" Ava asked, her face looking defeated.

"Yes," Aria paused for a moment to take in their haggard appearance a little more. "Stratton requested that I do this to keep the two of you safe."

"But how could you bring us back to that hell-hole?" Ava said, she looked as though she was going to burst into tears at any moment, her knuckles were bone white from clenching the edge of the table.

"You **know** that Maestro is a horrible place!" Katya said, clutching a fork like it was her lifeline. "And you ran away yourself, isn't this hypocritical?"

"Yes, it is hypocritical. But you don't know my reasons, nor will I tell you them. No. Project Maestro is safe. You don't understand how horrible the rest of the world is. People will rape or murder you to get the fancy Maestro electronics off of your unconscious body or corpse," Aria paused, looking at the two girls with fiery eyes. "The real world doesn't feed you; it will starve you in a heartbeat. And Fugue will always be after you."

The rest of the meal was eaten in silence. She understood that she had dashed their hopes of running away to be with each other, but she had done it to keep them safe. Yet that didn't bring her any comfort as the girls cried silently throughout the meal. They finished eating a little later; Aria started marching them back to Project Maestro. The two girls didn't voice any complaints, but she could see the mutinous stares from the two of them. She knew they would try to run away again, but she hoped they would have the sense not to try that in her presence. Aria didn't know enough about Fugue yet – and what she did know was in conflict. And even if she left, she doubted that she'd be able to get that far.

CHAPTER 17

Aria was sitting in Stratton's office. When she had arrived back at the facility with Ava and Katya in tow, he had told her to wait there so he could process the two girls. He needed to make sure they were still in good health and that they hadn't sustained any serious injuries from Fugue. He wasn't back yet and it had been several hours.

It wasn't the first time that she had been told to wait in his office. There were points after missions when she, Jinto, and Light had all waited together. Laughing at the memories they had gained during the trip. Not much had changed about his office. The heavy wood desk had a few more scratches on it, but was still coated with a decent amount of stray papers. The one picture on his desk still sat there, of a much younger Stratton with a beautiful young woman with long blonde hair and pale green eyes. Aria had looked at the picture many times, she didn't even have to squint to see the Adept tattoo on the woman's scalp. The woman was another of the staff members of Project Maestro – she had done a lot of work with recruiting. She had done all of the in-person interviews. Her name was Miss Marcellus, she had been one of the teachers as well.

Aria jumped as she heard the door unlock and saw Stratton walk in. He looked horrible. There were clear dark circles underneath his eyes and his clothes were more wrinkled than she had ever seen them. He was a military man through and through – his clothes were *always* crisp. He nodded at her as he rushed around to the other side of his desk and reached underneath it to pull out a half-empty bottle of whiskey. He didn't even bother with a glass this time. He took a large swig from the bottle before returning his attention to Aria.

"I'm very proud of you for bringing in these girls, Opus 1."

"*Proceed with caution. His flattery seems to have hidden motive.*"

"*Always does, Piano, always does.*"

"I'm glad that I was able to keep them out of danger from Fugue, but I'm not pleased that I brought them back to a place that doesn't allow them to be together, sir."

Aria's eyes dropped to her thighs. She remembered how Ava and Katya had looked when she brought them back, betrayal had been written on their faces. She had just been glad they hadn't tried to escape while she had brought them back; it would have been very hard to try to re-capture them. She wouldn't have wanted to.

"But you soldiered on through it. I commend you," he paused a second to take another swig from the bottle, his face barely registered that he had ingested alcohol. "I always knew that you would come back to your senses."

She scowled; the man didn't know why she had left.

"*Don't let him catch you off guard. He's saying it to rile you up, you know this,*" Piano said, his voice urgent.

"*I know. It's just...he's a very frustrating man.*"

Piano buzzed comfortingly in her mind, bringing a small grin to her face and strength to her body.

"I have another request for you, Opus 1."

As fast as the comfort from Piano had come, it was gone. Aria narrowed her eyes at him. She wanted to know why he was making requests rather than ordering her around. This wasn't how things worked.

"You're a smart girl. You can tell that I was gone longer than I needed to be. We were not able to bring Fugue back in. I was hoping to incarcerate them temporarily until we could play with their personalities a little more..." Aria watched him stare at his desk for a moment. "But I digress. The problem of Fugue has gotten out of hand."

Aria nodded in understanding. It was strange to see his face registering pain and helplessness.

"Fugue no longer follows my orders. It became apparent when they attacked Opus 6's bio cord. I figured that you and Opus 6 would return to Project Maestro in your own time; eventually the need for upgrades and medicine would outweigh your pride. I never ordered Fugue to bring the two of you back in. I *did* put up the wanted posters. I figured they would make you turn yourself in or go into hiding..." his voice trailed off; she swore that she heard his breath hitch. His face lost its vulnerability and became hard as stone. "I want you to eliminate the threat of Fugue. Opus 9 and 12 reported that Fugue tried to execute them before you got there and that the six of them attacked you all at once."

Aria nodded again, but she was confused. General Crawford, much less the rest of the government, would never authorize this. She pushed that to the back of her mind. While she had anticipating him asking for more help, she hadn't anticipated his openness. He was right; she and Light would have eventually come back to Project Maestro. Upgrades would have become necessary lest one of them end up with a shattered tibia from the stress of their muscles tightening more and more. She had anticipated that she would be the one having to deal with Fugue since the last time she had spoken to Stratton. She understood the threat that Fugue posed to the other Opera.

"Would I be able to work with my old team, sir? There are six Fugue members and only one of me. It would likely be safer if I worked with Opus 2 and Opus 6," Aria said, holding his gaze with ease. "But I don't know how I feel about killing Fugue. I don't want to kill for the government anymore." It was a bit of a bluff – she knew the government wouldn't authorize an Opus hunting down and killing Fugue. She just wanted more information.

Aria shivered under Stratton's cold, blue stare. It was like he was trying to see through her.

"What happened to you? I accepted earlier that you had discovered information that made you uncomfortable with your work at Project Maestro. I've wracked my brain trying to figure out *what* would cause you to change your mind. You *will* answer truthfully and *completely*. That is an order."

She choked on her breath, reached for the bottle that sat on Stratton's desk, and took a deep swig of the whiskey. It burned all the way down her throat, but she didn't care. Stratton looked like he was caught between outrage and horror.

"What the hell are we going to do?!"

"I advise that we answer truthfully. He doesn't seem in a tolerant mood."

"Uh, sorry. You caught me off guard," she said as her stomach churned with nerves. She didn't want to say the reason why she had left even if she had been ordered to do so. Even if she had known she would eventually have to do so. "Light, Jinto, and I had just finished off our marks and had met up at our designated meeting spot. As per usual for our missions, we hacked into the computer to see if there was any useful information, you know, if any countries were planning on attacking, which ones were planning on stopping trade. That kind of information," she paused, her face frozen in a troubled look. "We discovered *why* exactly the government had ordered these dignitaries be silenced. We discovered exactly what the government had done."

Stratton made a strangled sound, his blue eyes wider than Aria had ever seen them. She narrowed; his reaction made her believe that he had known this already. That didn't surprise her. He was military. The military had probably been in on it.

"The government ordered that the skies by scorched and blamed on another country. We had enough enemies to shove the blame on. I know that Project Maestro was created with the original purpose of hunting down people who had learned this secret, even if they weren't planning on divulging that information to the masses. We all had reservations about continuing our work after learning this information."

"His thoughts are all over the place, he's not even bothering to block me entirely."

The non-Adept staff members had learned to block the AIs very quickly, just like the Opera had been taught some basic maneuvers to keep Adepts from their minds. The fact that Stratton had dropped his defenses made Aria nervous. And it made her wonder *what* precisely he was thinking about.

She watched his face go back into an impassive mask, "I understand why you three had issues working for us after learning that. I understand that you might not want to kill for the government. Trust me when I say that I didn't want the skies to be scorched and that I did everything in my power to make sure that the government's plan would fail," he paused and held the bottle of whiskey contemplatively. "But you must understand that Fugue is an issue to your fellow Opera," he paused again, setting the bottle down to examine his fingernails. "I know that you don't want to take the lives of humans and AIs of Fugue. Just remember that Fugue is more complex than an Opus. They no longer have human identity and have a shared consciousness. They are neither human nor AI."

"*I don't like the idea of having to kill AIs, even if they're horribly corrupted.*"

"*I'm on the same page as you...but Fugue is a huge threat, especially with Opus having been declared a failure.*"

"That's right, discuss it with Piano," he smirked at her. "It's clear to me that Fugue is highly unhinged. It would be terrifying to see what would happen if they started targeting the general populace."

Aria glowered at Stratton; she hated when he was able to perceive what she was doing. Then again, he was in his position because he was able to read people. He worked with Opera almost every day of every single week of the past ten years. She shouldn't have been too surprised that he was able to tell when a host was speaking with their AI. What she said to Piano was her business, not

Stratton's. She shook away her irritation and focused on the second half of his statement. Fugue going after the general populace would be a catastrophe. At least the Opera would be able to attempt to fight them off. A normal person would not know what hit them.

Her shoulder's slumped in defeat, "I'll only kill them if its absolutely necessary. I will help you bring them in."

Aria felt sick to her stomach has she watched triumph blaze across Stratton's stressed face. He dismissed her and she left quickly.

CHAPTER 18

Aria had left almost immediately after agreeing to bring Fugue back in for Stratton. He had only asked her to eliminate the threat. Bringing them back in was one way to eliminate the threat without killing them. Before she had left, she and Piano had undergone another upgrade, one that Eli claimed would allow them to better find the Fugue members. She doubted that it would really help in the process of finding them, but she appreciated the gesture. Not all upgrades could be winners.

"*Any hints of them?*" Aria asked, looking around their surroundings carefully.

They had been following a near-cold trail for the past few hours and had found themselves in a relatively decent sized town by the name of Ironside. Like the Project Maestro facility, the city was partially built into one of the bluffs, but it wasn't for secrecy. It was for protection.

"*Not really. There are traces. They've definitely been here in the...last four days,*" Piano said, his voice dripped irritation. "*I don't really like this upgrade, its not very precise.*"

"*Maybe it'll clear up in a few days? Some of the past upgrades have taken a few days to fully sync with you.*"

Aria put her goggles over her eyes. They had been equipped with an upgraded heat vision that somehow could pinpoint when a person had an AI. The presence of an extra consciousness in the person's mind generated more heat than the average person and the head would glow white. It could also see heat traces on the ground and buildings and in rare cases in the air, but that wouldn't exactly tell her anything. Like the upgrade Piano had received, the one to her goggles seemed imprecise.

Sighing, she leaned against the wall. This was going nowhere. She had argued with Stratton about taking Light and Jinto with her, but he had said that Project Maestro needed the extra defense in case they were attacked by Fugue. She believed that to an extent – the place was a fortress, but like everything man made, it had weaknesses. Aria knew that the six had been playing with her when she retrieved Ava and Katya, seeing them fight at full strength would be a terrible sight. Stratton had also mentioned something about having three AIs going after Fugue would be foolish because they'd be easier to sense. They had also argued about the merit of killing Fugue – she had wanted to bring them in one by one. She would make it a different hell for them. Stratton had drilled into her mind that they were a hive mind, if that was so, she was going to make them be alone.

"*We should plug in, Piano,*" Aria whispered, her internal voice shaking. "*It's been far too long since we've seen each other.*"

Because this mission was off the books, so to speak, Aria hadn't been issued a laptop. They would have to search for a place to plug in.

"*I agree. We can also discuss what to do about Fugue.*"

"*Indeed.*"

Aria couldn't help but feel slightly disappointed that Piano was all business, as usual. They had been together for so long and had been through so much together that Piano felt like her best friend. The only one she could trust, ever.

He began directing her to the nearest computer source in Ironside, which was close for once. She entered the room with caution and wasn't surprised to see a thick layer of dust on top of the archaic tower. She slowly pulled the black cord from the back of her neck and plugged into the computer. She waited for the rush of transmitting to the digital world. And then she was surrounded by the clean, white world of Piano. While she felt slightly out of place in Piano's realm, it was still a comforting place. The silvery lines that resembled circuitry that ran through everything would not hurt her. The air was humming with digital signals would not harm her.

She strode over to Piano, who was standing with his hands in his pockets looking more relaxed than she had seen him in ages. She gave him a brief embrace, her way of showing gratitude for him saving her so many times. He lingered in her arms a little loner than usual; it had been a trying few weeks. Both of them had come close to death several times.

Aria didn't know what to say to him, though. While Piano was her dearest friend, he had hidden a vital part of their history for years, and she wasn't sure how she felt about that. The fact that she had almost died. But she knew that now wasn't the time to dwell on that. Now was the time to relax a little before they had more work to do. She stretched out on the floor.

"We need to deal with Fugue, Aria. This tracking upgrade that they gave us...it sucks. There's no way that it'll be able to find them."

"Well, at least they upgraded my goggles as well? Heat vision is pretty neat. Although, it'll only really work if they're right in front of our faces. We know how they look. I don't need a heat scan to confirm who they are. It's not like they have a powerful Adept on their side."

She had heard a long time ago that exceptionally powerful Adepts could warp the appearance of themselves and those around them.

Piano lay down on the digital ground with Aria. His head was next to hers, their hair blending together to make a pink and brown fan. What seemed like moments of companionable silence passed between the two of them, but the digital world warped time and it actually could have been several hours that passed.

"I think they gave us an impossible task, Piano. We will never succeed. We're on their tail, yes, but how will we be able to make up the distance that they've put between us?"

"We'll find them. We never really did work as a tracking unit, but we can track. We will do this for the good of the other Opera. We won't let Fugue start going after normal people, either."

Aria felt troubled. The greater good frightened her. She didn't want to be a martyr for the greater good. Killing Fugue wasn't for the greater good, it was for Stratton. It was to coverup the fact that they no longer responded to his orders.

"But we're just covering Maestro's tracks. I hate that we're dong missions again..." Aria said, glad that the digital realm didn't allow her to cry, but her eyes burned all the same. "After what we learned..."

"I know. But imagine what Fugue would do to the general population. You heard their voices...the...hatred..."

Aria didn't want to think about what they would do, but the thoughts started anyway. Fugue was unhinged. It was easy to see that. Hundreds, thousands of people could die for no reason. Piano was right, they couldn't allow that to happen.

"I see what you mean, Piano. I know that my plan was to bring them back one by one, but they're so far ahead. It doesn't feel like there's a good way to go about this anymore."

"I know, but we always figure out a way."

Aria fell silent again. He was right again. Piano was always right like that. She pulled her knees to her chest. The whole Fugue thing had her off-balance. She was weirded out by Stratton asking her for help instead of demanding it. She was lost without her teammates. And she missed Babylon. She knew that she needed to keep pressing forward, but she just didn't want to start moving again.

"We'll stick to the original plan. Bringing them in one by one. It'll throw them off guard. They like working as a group as much as an Opus likes working by themselves."

She heard Piano hesitate, but couldn't bring herself to look at him, "But what if there's more than one of them?"

"Knock out the others, return one. If the situation calls for it, I might be forced to kill one. It'll take a long time, but it feels like its our only option."

She didn't want to admit it, but Aria sounded exactly like she had when she was an Opus on assassination missions. She had been forced to become a cold killing machine lest she think about who her mark had been too much. She remembered her first kill, she hadn't separated herself from the situation and had needed awhile to recover emotionally from the mission. Light and Jinto had been the same way. She still hadn't forgiven herself for that first kill or some of the more questionable missions.

"I know what you're thinking of, Aria. You're always going to be Aria to me. The girl that introduced herself and asked questions. Always curious and always sweet. That's who you are to me. Even when you were working for Project Maestro," Piano said gently.

Too many memories flooded her mind. Old missions she had done with Light and Jinto. Meeting Piano. Stratton scaring the living daylights out of all the original Opera. The Madeline she remembered, the sweet little girl she had left behind. That mark's eyes, soft and pleading. Begging her to not go through with what she had been ordered to do. The sickening crack of his neck breaking followed by her own sobs.

"I know that's who I am to you. But I really don't feel that way."

She managed to give Piano a shaky smile before removing herself from the digital world. She needed to time to sort through her memories, time to think on her own. It was time for a shower. She didn't care how much time had passed at this point – they would pick up Fugue's trail again. They had orders.

CHAPTER 19

The shower always cleared Aria's mind. She had always been a realistic thinker, but she sounded too pessimistic to be herself. The past few weeks were hanging heavily in her mind. She needed to focus on who she was now and what she needed to get done in the next few days. Dwelling on the past would only make everything harder at this point.

"Sorry that I ran off, Piano. I needed to think."

Piano buzzed around her mind before saying, *"It's alright. Our lives have practically turned upside down the past few weeks. It's been a lot to swallow. For both of us."*

He was right, life outside of Project Maestro had always been a little rough around the edges, even when they had been in Night City. She had managed to make money, but often ended up going back to this universe to do jobs and visit people. That had continued on for three years. Every once and awhile she would run into another Opera or just a plain old Project Maestro operative. She had been so confused by the operative that was tailing her so well. They had made it impossible to go back to Night City with how closely they were tailing her. She just didn't feel comfortable trying to hop a bus with them dogging her. Aria just wanted life to be what it had been before Fugue had come into play. Life had been tough, but it had been manageable. Now there were too many variables out of Aria's control. She was back to being a pawn rather than her own person.

"*We should get moving again. Do you sense anything about their trail?*" Aria said while she slipped on and laced her boots.

"*A little. They went west, it seems. We're in luck, there's a decent sized road that we should be able to go on.*"

"*I'm assuming we're still four days behind them?*"
"*Yes.*"

"*Well, nothing we can do to change that except moving faster than they do. Let's head west.*"

Aria left the building that they had hidden in and glanced up at the sky. The orange was rotting into brown – night was falling. A small smile stretched across her face. She liked traveling under darkness, it might allow them to be able to catch up to Fugue. Usually on official Opus missions, they tended to travel during the day, unless they were hard-pressed for time. Once she had left Project Maestro she had learned the benefits of traveling at night out of necessity.

She stretched down and tapped the button on the sides of her boots that turned them into skates. The feel of four wheels under each foot comforted her a little and chased away the demons that were crawling around her mind. Aria pushed off hard with her left leg and felt the skates' power kick in and propel her forward. It was a sensation that she had come to love; the surging forward, the wind on her face, and her hair whipping around her. The speed made her feel like she had never heard the codename Fugue before.

The dwindling light continued as she was traveling west, but soon it was too dark to see further than two feet in front of her face. She lowered her goggles over her eyes and tapped one of the many buttons on the sides. The night vision kicked in and she was able to see like it was daylight again. Aria just hoped that she wouldn't encounter any lights; she had learned the hard way that the night vision setting meant just that, for night only. Any exposure to light temporarily blinded her. They didn't have time for that.

"How's the trail feeling?"

"A little better, but still not good. I can tell they were here. It's like little bits of their essence gets left where they go. I can faintly feel it on you from when you fought them. But they're not going to be in the next town. I'm guessing we're about two hours behind them now."

"Yeah...my gut didn't think they'd be in the next town either. Too easy. And for as much as they know about us, we don't know much about them."

Aria kept her speed up while skating, if they were catching up, she wanted to continue that trend.

"This is very true," Piano said, he hesitated a moment. *"Though, if we're catching up so easily, its quite possible that they **might** be in the next town..."*

"*I don't know, Piano. I'm the only Opus who goes to small towns to hide out, not counting Katya and Ava. They weren't thinking things through. I would assume that Fugue would hide out in a larger town, somewhere with the resources to support six people who have AIs,*" she stopped abruptly, she thought something had skittered in front of her. There was nothing there. Aria shook her head a few times. "*Ugh, I'm getting paranoid. When we come up on the first town, we'll do a quick scan. If anything pops up, we'll examine it.*"

Piano agreed with her. She took a few deep breaths and tried to get her pulse back to normal. The whole situation had her way too jumpy. Most roads were abandoned at night, especially in this area of the country. She'd be more concerned if she were on either coast. She had gotten many a scar from night traveling on the coasts. She pushed off once she was calmed down.

It didn't take them long to reach the small town. From the outskirts, Aria could see that they had the basics – living facilities, a store or two, and government guards. She was thankful that the road they were on didn't cut through the town. Even though she had her Project Maestro issued ID with her, she didn't want to deal with guards. They did a brief scan of the city. Piano reported that their signatures were all over the place, but that they were at least a day or two old.

"*At least we're going the right direction. Do you know of any cities in this direction?*"

"*Scanning.*"

She hated that Project Maestro was located in the middle of nowhere; it was a moderately long trip to any of the surrounding towns and cities. Most times an Opus was traveling on foot, be it by walking or skating. Vehicles were hard to come by, even for a program like Project Maestro.

"*About two hours away, maybe less if you push yourself. Want to set that as the destination?*"

"*Yes.*"

Even though they weren't going through the town, Aria slowed down her skating. She didn't want to draw attention to herself and rocketing through the town was a surefire way to draw unneeded and unwanted attention. Once she hit the other side of the town, she pushed off hard once again to get the speed going. She would need the speed to catch up to Fugue, especially since the city was at least two hours away.

After a little more than an hour and a half of hard skating, they were at the edge of the city. The city was dark, but the street lights cast an eerie yellow glow against the battered street. She tapped a button to turn off her night vision and one more to turn on her heat vision. The usual lights popped up, showing general signs of life. Nothing was as bright as it needed to be, but there were a few promising spots. It gave her a small amount of hope, but hope didn't go far with her.

"*I'm not getting much...what do you sense, Piano?*"

"*There's...there's only one of them. The rest are gone. One of them is definitely in this city.*"

Aria couldn't help but feel happy that she had managed to find one, but a bitter taste filled her mouth. It seemed weird to only find one though. They were supposed to need to be in a group to function properly. She shook away the feeling and thoughts; and reminded herself that this wasn't for Project Maestro. This was for the greater good of the Opera and for the general population. She followed the directions that Piano had given her. She was unfamiliar with the city they were in, she didn't eve know the name. Strange considering its close proximity to Project Maestro. Most of the jobs she had taken in the three years she was away from Maestro had been much further south, or on the coasts. She had stayed as far away from Project Maestro as she could. Getting out of the former United States was near impossible – the borders between Mexico and Canada had been shut for years.

They came up on a dilapidated building; it was similar to the buildings she had favored when she was working. It didn't seem like a building that a Fugue member would ever hide in.

"*Are you sure this is the building? Doesn't seem like something Fugue would hide in.*"

"*I'm positive. The scans are showing that, undeniably, one of them is hiding in the upper right room.*"

She shrugged and moved closer to the building. She easily climbed up a drain pipe that went by the window next to the room the Fugue operative was supposedly hiding in. She breathed out heavily, stealth bored her at times, even if they were good at it. But boring was safe and she and Piano needed to stay safe. She crawled through the window silently; she couldn't afford to be heard at this point, it could screw up the entire mission. Fugue members were too good at disappearing. She set herself onto the floor as gently as possible, her arms were shaking from the exertion. She was pleased to see that there was carpet instead of a the unpleasantly familiar thick layer of dust. Aria pushed to her feet and looked around. The outside of the building had deceived her. It was clear that Fugue had stayed here for a while – it was well furnished. It was clear that this had been a bedroom for one of the other members. She tried to make her way over to the door without making a noise, but the building proved its age and creaked with her first step.

She heard scuffling from the room next to her, but it wasn't running away, it was running towards her. That confused her, maybe the operative was expecting the rest of Fugue to come back. If that was the case, she would need to hurry. She shrugged and sneaked behind the swinging door to get ready for a surprise attack. She shifted down onto her haunches, coiled like a spring. The operative rushed in, her long silvery hair billowing behind her. She looked around frantically trying to locate the source of the creak. Aria leaped at her and wrapped an arm around her mouth and held her tight against her body. The operative found for a few moments, but went limp.

She simply stopped fighting. Aria dropped the girl to the ground, disappointed and relieved all at once. She had hoped that the girl would put up a little more fight, but an easy capture was always preferable.

"What do you want" The operative said, hunched over on the ground. Aria was having trouble remembering the girl's name.

"Stratton sent me to eliminate the threat of Fugue to keep the Opus program safe. I'm bringing you back to Project Maestro. They will deal with you there."

"I'll never go with you. I need my brothers and sisters..."

Aria looked at the girl a little closer, she was close to hysterics, and not because an enemy had waltzed into her base of operations. She looked lost and confused. The last time Aria had seen the girls she had looked entirely together and in control; the stark difference was enough to shake the usually unflappable Aria. She reached out and put a hand on the girl's shoulder, which was shaking with suppressed sobs. The girl slapped Aria's arm away and glowered up at her.

"What's your name?" Aria asked gently, sitting down on the floor with her.

"They call me Elegy."

"*I know what you're playing at Aria, its pointless. Stratton said that they're no longer aware of their human selves. Fugue is just a cluster of AIs that have full control over human bodies.*"

"*Human consciousness just doesn't cease to exist. You can't destroy data.*"

"What was your name before you came to Project Maestro?" Aria said, pointedly ignoring Piano.

Her AI expressed his displeasure by thrashing around in her mind a little. She schooled her expression into indifference, despite the pain he was causing.

Elegy's face went blank as she stared at Aria and sadness and confusion seemed to radiate from her, "They call me Elegy...but I think I had a name before Fugue. But why would I want a name other than Elegy? Where are my brothers and sisters?"

"*Aria, just bring her in. This is getting creepy. I'm sensing almost pure AI.*"

"Almost isn't all. There had to be some human left in her. Can't you feel that sadness?"

"*Well, yes, but it feels more residual than genuine!*" he thrashed around a few more times.

Aria ignored the pain, she refused to believe him. She knew that an AI could take full control of the host. Piano had done it for her when she was too tired to move without assistance. But Elegy was more like a human shell. They had been told that the strength of their AI would grow the more they interacted. The Fugue AIs were powerful, there *had* to have been interaction. She wanted to believe that Stratton would have said no to this project, but the blank stare from Elegy told her otherwise. There seemed to be a large possibility that he might have stolen the humanity from six teenagers.

Aria pushed the thoughts away and sat down with Elegy on the floor, like they were equals. Elegy eyed her cautiously, like Aria was doing something entirely foreign and wrong.

"Tell me about Fugue, Elegy." There was a hint of danger weaved in her voice. The girl was confused and distraught enough that she might not need any physical persuasion to talk.

Elegy peered over at Aria, her green eyes narrowed in suspicion, "Most information on Fugue is classified."

"It's been apparent to me that Fugue doesn't seem to care about chain of command or anything like that. Why obey the classified order?" Aria paused for a second, a small smirk playing across her lips. "And I'm Opus 1. I almost assuredly have the clearance."

Most of the Opera had decent clearance. Not the best, of course. The government had many secrets, as Aria had discovered. But between the fact that all of the Opera were instructed to get as much information as possible when on jobs and the fact that they were all frighteningly intelligent – it was just easier for the government to give them *some* clearance. It was better than the alternative of Opera always hacking into the databases.

Elegy looked conflicted for a moment, before shrugging and leaning back against the wall,

"Fugue is my family. Fugue will always be my family."

"Did you have a family before Fugue?"

"*Aria, this is futile.*"

The clipped tone of this voice made her realize how far she was pushing him.

"*Piano, just let me talk to the girl. It's too late to head back to Maestro tonight; might as well make some small talk.*"

He made a small sound of irritation. Every once and awhile Aria decided to ignore his advice and do her own thing; which he absolutely hated. They were a team. She was aware that Piano felt like she was betraying their team when she did things like this. A moment later she felt him buzz, she took that as acceptance.

"...Family..." Elegy whispered, her head falling to her knees. "Once I had a family. I think...I think my name was Elena. Or maybe that's just Elegy playing tricks..."

Aria quirked her eyebrow toward her hairline, "Your AI can play tricks?"

"I *am* Elegy. I think I used to be Elena."

"Well...Elena...we've got about three hours until sunrise. Why don't you get some sleep. We can't leave for Project Maestro at this time of night. I'll keep watch for your wonderful family. And to be safe, I'm tying your wrists," she said, with a bright smile. She was tired of trying to get information from the girl. She had to hand it to Project Maestro – whatever they had done to

Fugue made it damn near impossible to get information out of them.

Elegy looked at her, eyes even narrower, and nodded slowly. Aria felt relieved, she didn't think that this one would try and run away from her; she seemed to be too lost and confused to think. It seemed that the girl who might have been named Elena was entirely lost to Fugue. Just thinking that chilled her to the bone.

CHAPTER 20

Aria was thankful that she had only given Elegy three hours to rest up. Memories and the thought of AIs taking over humans had occupied her mind the whole time she was keeping guard for the rest of Fugue. She leaned against the wall and glanced over at Elegy, the girl was still sleeping soundly. She shook her head; her parents had sent her and Madeline to the government despite knowing how corrupt it was. Her mother had been a doctor, her father had worked for a successful high tech electronics shop. They had both dealt with the government extensively. And it wasn't a secret that the government was shady.

It troubled Aria that she was thinking of before she had Piano. She couldn't imagine what life would be like now if she didn't have him, but she could remember how simple life had been before Project Maestro had barged into her life. She had studied and danced, she had eaten dinner with her family. Sometimes she found herself longing for that life back, if only for that simplicity. Yet the mere thought of being without Piano made her never want to change the present or the past. She was bitter about some of the things she had been forced to do and she would be for a long time. Life without her AI seemed bleak.

Aria remembered when she had first been implanted with Piano, thirteen years old and completely confused and frightened. She had woken up in the medical ward, disoriented and weak, but alive. Aria had been able to feel something new in her mind, but it wasn't invasive. It was like that they just added intelligence to her mind. She had felt complete. Piano had explained who he was and what his purpose was. He had expressed concern at her being so very young. He had eased her through her confusion, which had helped them bond as she was slowly able to move around. He had become her most trusted friend almost immediately. She couldn't imagine what life would be like without him. Sure, there had been plenty of awkward moments. Her first kiss, which had been with Light. The first time she had sex, which had been with Jinto. Their AIs had all mentioned it being incredibly awkward – she didn't blame them. Even with that, she didn't want to imagine what life would be like without her AI.

"*We should get on the road, Aria,*" he said, he sounded tired. "*Are you alright? You seem troubled again.*"

"*I'll be fine once we're moving. I had too much time to think last night.*"

She glanced out the window, he was right. The sun was starting to rise. There were shadows dancing over Elegy's sleeping figure. She sighed and went to wake her up. Elegy was surprisingly easy to wake and nodded as Aria explained that it was time to head back. Her stomach knotted with suspicion with how agreeable Elegy was being, but she pushed it from her mind. She needed to stay focused. She untied the girl's hands and threatened that she could cut Elegy's hands off if she tried to run away.

Aria and Elegy started making their way towards Project Maestro. It was going to be a long journey, especially since Elegy hadn't been equipped with electronic roller blades. She figured it wouldn't be too bad if they didn't stop often, they were Project Maestro operatives. They were stronger than a normal human and had better endurance as well. If they made good time they might be able to make it back by dusk. She knew it would go fastest if she carried the girl on back and just used her skates; but Aria flat out refused to do that.

"I need to stop," Elegy said, not even bothering to bring her eyes up to Aria's.

If it hadn't been the fourth time they had stopped in an hour and a half, Aria would have been more gracious, "Again? Really?"

The girl shrugged and plopped down on the side of the industrialized road to have a rest that would, no doubt, last about ten to twenty minutes. Aria had to wonder if Fugue operatives were designed to be more short range than an Opus was – she wasn't feeling the strain of the journey yet. She knew that it didn't make sense for Fugue to be considered short distance. Most missions that Project Maestro operatives went on were long range – the facility was almost literally in the middle of nowhere. She understood that Elegy might be stalling. Aria hadn't been enthusiastic to return to Project Maestro after disobeying Stratton's orders. She knew that whatever awaited the girl wasn't pleasant.

"Alright, that's enough rest," Aria said while reaching down to pull Elegy to her feet. "I want to get back to the facility by dusk. We're going to have to make good time on the rest of our trip to do that."

Elegy said nothing, but sent Aria the fiercest glare she had seen in quite some time. She was amused for a brief moment when she wondered if Taranis could out-glare Elegy. The amusement melted away as the girl's gaze went blank. Elegy was possibly the worst travel companion that Aria had ever had. It felt like ants were crawling in her skin when Elegy's face went blank.

"She's creeping me out."

"I can tell. The fact that she doesn't have much humanity left is showing."

Deep down she knew that Piano was right – even though she didn't want to admit that. She wanted to believe that Project Maestro was too noble to take humanity away from six people. They must have caught Elegy in a rare moment when whatever was left of the host was more in control. Sometimes Aria wondered how she had managed to survive as an assassin; she was far too idealistic at times.

It wasn't very much after dusk when they arrived at gates of Project Maestro. To Aria, the trip had been relatively uneventful, much more like babysitting than transporting a dangerous operative. For the first time, the hidden monolith Maestro building seemed like a warm welcome. They approached the gates in the standard method, their hands in the air to show that they meant to harm. As they got closer, Aria noticed that the building was in partial lock-down mode. There were flashing red lights on the lowered gates and the guards in the booth looked shaken and pale. She immediately dismissed that this was a drill; even the newest guards were professional enough to not show their fear during a drill.

"Opus I requesting entrance. I am escorting Elegy of the Fugue department," she said in her best authoritative voice.

"J-just a s-second Opus I, le-let me call th-this in," the guard said. She wasn't sure if he normally stuttered or if he was just that frightened.

Aria nodded in understand as she listened to his quick, panicked voice. She couldn't quite make out what he was saying, something she knew was deliberate. One of the guards was an Adept and he was screwing with her perception of the words. Something had happened. She shifted her hands from above her head and grabbed Elegy's arm into the escort position. She had declared who she was, now it was time to worry about her potentially dangerous captive.

"*Piano, what do you think is happening in there?*"

"*...I'll see if I can dig anything up...*" her AI's voice was shaking.

The fact that the building was in partial lockdown mode made her feel troubled. Aria had very little love for Project Maestro, but she didn't want people to be hurt. They would be unnecessary casualties – that, and she had grown up and trained with them for so long. She wanted the other Opera to be safe. She didn't want the guards hurt, they had only had the misfortune of being assigned to this post. She didn't want anyone to be hurt.

"Alright, seems like we can let you in, follow me please," the bolder guard said and motioned for her to follow.

Aria complied and jerked Elegy along with her to the entrance of Project Maestro. The doors had the solid steel blast doors slammed shut. She furrowed her eyebrows, those doors being down was a very bad thing. Nothing about the situation was sitting well with her.

"*Aria, something is very wrong here.*"

"*I was thinking the exact same thing. I don't think the blast doors have ever been down before – I've only ever read about them being able to go down.*"

The guard punched in a code and Aria watched the blast doors lift; as they did, the acrid sent of burning electronics and hair flooded Aria's nostrils. The lobby of the facility was charred black and broken. She could see blood spattered on the walls. The Adept guard seemed to tense, gave her a sad look, and ran away.

"No..."

Aria turned her gaze to Elegy. The girl's face was twisted into a strange grin and there was a gleam in her eyes that had definitely not been there before. Elegy looked straight at her, her bright green eyes full of life.

"Always together, never to part, Fugue will finish what Opus starts..." Elegy whispered, raising her arm to throw a punch.

Aria stopped the momentum from the punch by pushing Elegy's shoulder back. She flinched when she heard the joint crack. She knew that sort of injury hurt, but it didn't slow down her opponent. Elegy viciously grabbed at Aria's throat, she stopped her by throwing a strong front kick to Elegy's shin and started backing her into the corner with continuing strikes. She felt Piano meld into her limbs, becoming her second set of eyes and reflexes. She grimaced as a blow slipped through both of their watchful eyes and grazed her cheekbone. Aria continued backing Elegy into the corner, but Elegy was blocking almost all the strikes and countering often enough that Aria was hurting.

"Aria, be careful, it feels like she's luring you into a trap. She can clearly keep up with you."

"I know Piano...but what happened here? Why is there blood on the walls?!"

Aria grabbed Elegy by the injured shoulder and tossed her at the wall, "Back off Elegy, I don't want to hurt you," she snarled as she dropped her fighting stance.

"Fugue will eliminate the problem of Opus!" Elegy said while grabbing Aria's hair.

"Damn it!"

Aria kicked Elegy's shins as hard as she could and almost took pride in the scream that escaped from Elegy's throat. She could hear memories replaying in her mind, but she squashed them away. Now was now the time for that. Elegy let go of Aria's hair and was bent over, panting like a dog on a hot day. Aria stood above her, her eyes cold despite the hot anger and frustration that was flowing through her veins.

"*Aria, keep cool. If you lose your temper, you're going to lose this fight.*"

"*I...I know. I just want to know what's going on...*"

"*I haven't been able to dig up anything, I'm sorry.*"

Piano buzzed in her mind comfortingly and Aria managed to relax a little. Elegy lunged at her, sending her flying into a wall. Her head was spinning. Elegy's weight was on her chest and she could feel her face being punched over and over. Aria had been right about them toying with her – they were far stronger than they had been letting on.

"*Piano...help me!*"

She felt him take over her body and throw Elegy off of her. She slammed back into her control and slowly stood up, cracking her neck and knuckles, trying desperately to shake the dizziness that clouded her throbbing head. Aria needed the fight to be done, she wouldn't be able to continue it for much longer, not with a possible concussion. Her vision was swimming – she was done trying to subdue rather than hurt. She lifted Elegy up into the air by her shirt and kicked her underneath the jaw, knocking her unconscious. She dropped her back to the ground and reached into her messenger bag for something to restrain her with.

"That wasn't the fight I had been anticipating. She was entirely different than she was the entire trip. More evidence that they're playing some sick game," Aria said while binding Elegy's wrists together. *"Ugh, my head is killing me..."*

"Not surprised. That was a nasty hit you took. Its been a long time since you asked me for help like that."

He was right, it had been a long time since she had needed help like that in a fight. Aria looked at massive scar on her right arm, if she remembered right, that day was the last time Piano had needed to help her to that extent. She shook away those thoughts and started sprinting towards the Opera wing. She needed to see what had happened; she needed to make sure that Madeline, all of them, were all right.

CHAPTER 21

The run to the Opera wing had never seemed to take Aria so long. As she got closer, the amount of charring on the walls got darker, the blood spatter more obvious. She only hoped that there had been no casualties, even though her common sense was telling her that the amount of blood on the walls meant that someone had died. She just didn't want to believe it.

"Piano do you sense any of the other Opera?"

"I feel faint AIs...I'd say that the hosts are injured or..."

"Please don't say it Piano, please..."

Aria skidded to a halt in front of doors that were most definitely locked. She wasn't surprised to find the Opera wing in partial lock-down mode either, but it was frustrating. There weren't any guards at the check point, so he and Piano would have to hard-wire the door to let her in. She was thankful that the blast door wasn't down. She wouldn't be able to do anything to get that up until the partial-lock down was lifted. She approached the door with caution, she knew that Piano would be proud of her. Rushing in could get her shocked and knocked unconscious. She couldn't afford that at the moment. She pulled the panel next to the door off and looked at all the colorful wiring. Aria sighed; working with electronics had been one of her weaknesses. She had always let Light or Jinto deal with electrical work.

"Which wires pair up?"

"You still don't remember how to do this?" Aria could hear amusement mixing with irritation in Piano's voice.

"Do you think now is the appropriate time to make fun of my lackluster electronics skills?"

She heard Piano laugh in her mind, *"I suppose not. Green to red, orange to black, blue to purple."*

Aria did as Piano told her to do and was happy to hear the buzz of electricity enter the door. She tapped the open button and watched the doors swing open for her. She rushed through them, but hesitated at the sight of severely scorched walls. One of the walls had a huge crack running through it and there blood trails that continued toward the habitation wing. It was clear that the Opera wing had been the target. The guards that were supposed to be manning the door were slumped on the ground. Aria didn't know if they were dead or alive, but she didn't have time to check. She sighed and started running again, picking up the blistering pace she had set before.

As she made her way into the Opera habitation wing, she felt tears well in her eyes. The place that had been her home for so many years was in ruins. There was rubble blocking the doorway to her old room. There shouldn't have been anyone in there. She didn't want to know how the walls were cracked, how a sturdy facility like Project Maestro was this damaged. She didn't want to know what sort of power it took to do that. Aria reached up to her ear and felt the communication device sitting there, silent. She had to wonder why they hadn't used it – she would have been able to help defend Project Maestro. She walked down the hallway, looking for any indication as to what had really happened.

"Ari...is that you?" a familiar voice said from further down the hallway. "Andante can feel you...but I can't see you yet..."

Aria ran to the voice and found Jinto half buried under rubble, his glasses shattered on the floor next to him. Her stomach knotted up, he looked so frail. There was blood trickling down his face from a gash on his forehead. He looked like he was in excruciating pain. She knelt down next to him and brushed his hair out of the wound on his forehead. She looked at the rubble that was covering him and saw that he was very fortunate. There was a lot of twisted steel and stone covering him, but the largest pieces were off to either side of him.

"What happened to you, Jinto?"

"Fugue attacked...not all of them, though. They were missing one of their members."

"I know. I found her in a city about six hours away. She tried to kill me...she's unconscious and tied up in the lobby," Aria said as she started to move the rocks and steel to release him.

"We had been given some time to just relax for the first time in a long time, so we were all separate. The five of them started to go after one Opera at a time, but we figured out what was going on and started ganging up on them. They had done enough damage beforehand to really cripple our forces. I know Keiran was out of the fight before we all teamed up, Ava as well. There were a lot of injuries, but I don't know if there were any casualties," Jinto said, barely stifling a groan as he stretched his now free arms.

"Piano, scan for the Fugue AIs please."

It didn't take Aria long to move enough rubble to free Jinto entirely. She stood up next to him, holding a hand out to him, "Alright, can you move your legs?" He nodded stiffly. "Then lets get you to your feet and get you to the medical ward, okay?"

Her friend leaned heavily on her shoulder, his whole body shaking with the exertion of standing. She laced her left arm under his arms and supported his weight the best she could while she was wobbling from her own injuries.

"I don't sense any of them but Elegy and she appears to be unconscious. Maybe some of them were killed in action?"

"Somehow I don't think we were that lucky."

"I don't know if Dr. Taranis is there. Fugue might have killed her," Jinto said as he bit back a cry of pain.

"They need Taranis alive. She specializes in helping people with AIs. It's clear that she helped

Eli design the upgrades for all of us," she paused for a second and added. "It would be smarter for them to kidnap her in case any of their members were injured."

If Fugue had kidnapped Taranis, the Opera were screwed. If Jinto's injuries were an indication of how bad the fight had gone, things were bad. He was trying to hide the extent of his injuries from Aria, but she had known him long enough to know that he was in pain. They walked through the hallways and she was both relieved and anxious to see that the damage and destruction became less as they got closer to the medical ward.

"When did all of this happen?" Aria said as she winced. Jinto wasn't too heavy, but she was dealing with the injuries she had sustained fighting Elegy. The terrain they were moving through didn't hep the situation either.

"Fugue minus one ambushed the Project Maestro facility this afternoon. It happened so fast...I was catching up on some reading. I heard Holly scream for help, and then we were all out of our rooms fighting..."

There was something about the entire situation that didn't sit well with Aria. She leaves to bring Fugue back in and the Opera wing gets savaged. It troubled her that it seemed like Stratton had sent her on mission just so she would be out of the way.

"Stop that line of thinking. Right now. This isn't Stratton's style. This is way too unorganized. It seems that Fugue was lucky. Jinto said that the rest of the Opera were enjoying a relaxing afternoon for the first

time in a long time. Had they been in training, I think Fugue would have been annihilated."

Aria bit her lip a little, she knew that he was right, *"I still need to talk to him and ask why I wasn't pulled in."*

The question of how Fugue got in was a non-issue. Each of the Opera knew many different ways to get into the facility – even if Fugue hadn't been around as long, they would surely know a few ways to get in.

A few minutes later, they arrived at the medical ward. The beds were full of Opera in various states of injury. It broke her heart to see people she had grown up with and had taken care of in such critical condition. Taranis ran up, her golden hair was frazzled, but she seemed relieved to see that two more Opera had shown up. She helped Aria walk Jinto to a bed and sat him down. He winked at her and held her hand for a few extra seconds.

"Thanks very much for bringing him here," Taranis said while ushering Aria away from the bed and motioning for one of her nurses to start taking care of Jinto. "Where did you find him?"

"Half-buried in rubble in the habitation units for the Opera. He was lucky, but I doubt he would have made it through the night."

"I'm harder to get rid of than that," Jinto said with a pained smile.

"You're probably right. We were going to send out a search party for him soon," Taranis said, ignoring Jinto entirely. She then paused a moment to take a closer look at Aria. Her eyes narrowed. "You're injured. Badly."

Aria rolled her eyes and glowered down at the doctor, "I'm fine. You have more important things to deal with at the moment," she hesitated a moment before continuing. "But...I need to know. Were there any casualties?"

"Unfortunately, yes."

Aria's heart felt as though it had stopped beating. Someone had died. She felt her face go slack. She didn't want to hear who it as, but knew that she needed to know.

"M-May I ask who?"

"Well, it's not your younger sister, she's in the bed over there," Taranis said while pointing to her left.

Aria glanced over at Madeline, she was curled on the left side of her body holding her stomach. She could see that there was a cast on her sister's arm and that her face was bruised.

"Ma'am, please, this isn't a joking matter. These people are my friends.

Taranis sighed and looked Aria straight in the eye, "Opus 6 passed away about an hour and a half ago from severe internal and external injuries. The other members told me he was incredibly brave and is the reason the rest of them are alive."

Aria fell to her knees. Light was gone. One of her only friends was gone. One of her best friends was dead. Taranis pointed towards a bed surrounded by curtains at the very back of the ward and told Aria that that's here he was if she wanted to see him. She pulled at her short hair, this couldn't have happened. She and Light were the ones that had escaped Project Maestro. An Opus didn't let their emotions get the better of them. She swallowed any sorrow she had and schooled her face into a blank stare. Her body was trembling, the only indication that she was feeling *something.*

Once her body had stopped shaking, she pushed herself to her feet, almost embarrassed that she had fallen to the floor. Aria walked towards the bed in the back of the ward while Piano buzzed in her mind, trying to bring her any consolation. She could feel her AI's concern, she wasn't herself. No. Right now she was entirely Opus 1. Light's body was on the bed, his eyes closed. It almost looked like he was sleeping. The fire that she had always associated with Light was gone; his hair didn't even seem to be as red. Everything that had made him Light was gone; but she couldn't believe that human consciousness could just cease to exist. Guilt settled deep in her stomach. It was her fault that her best friend was dead. If she hadn't gone and bothered him about the wanted posters that Stratton had put up, he would still be alive. He would still be safe in his fortress.

Aria turned away from his body, she couldn't look at it anymore. Piano was whispering words of condolence to her, but they didn't comfort her. She wanted to make Fugue pay for what they had done. She wanted to hurt them for killing Light.

For hurting Madeline, Jinto, and the rest of the Opera. Aria wanted revenge.

CHAPTER 22

Aria leaned back on the bed that Taranis had forced her to sit on. She wasn't allowed to leave until Stratton spoke with her. She had never been a fan of medical type places, they made her freak out. They smelled like artificial clean that barely covered the scent of blood and sick people. And when she added in that the medical ward was full of injured Opera and Light's corpse, she found that she was even more on edge. Every once and awhile she glanced over at Madeline's bed. Her sister was clearly awake, but seemed to be in too much pain to actually move. Seeing her sister in that bed made her feel like she was a bad older sister.

She didn't want to sit still, so she went to stand up to pace around the room. Taranis glared at Aria and pointed at the bed. The injuries were worse than she had thought they were. Her concussion alone was causing more problems than she liked. When she stood up, everything would spin for a moment before coming to a stop. Even when the world wasn't spinning, it was skewed. Everything had been fine until she had stopped moving.

"Aria, they call that adrenaline," Piano said, a hint of condescension creeping into his voice.

"*I know. I knew I had taken some injuries, but I thought I was fine.*"

"*The way Elegy was fighting you I'm surprised you took so **little** damage,*" Piano whispered, falling back into his quiet role. "*She pulled some nasty tricks.*"

"*Yes, she did. But they were smart moves, but I'll admit to disliking having my hair pulled,*" Aria said while leaning back against the pillow. "*I'm glad that we ended up fighting her, though. She's vicious. I think there would have been more damage to the Opera if she had been fighting them.*"

"*I think you may be right.*"

Aria watched Taranis get Jinto to his feet and hand him a polished black cane. He looked disgusted for a moment, but a sharp glance from the woman made him grab the cane without hesitation. Taranis held his right arm as he took the cane in his left hand and helped him walk around the room a little. He was one of the few Opera who was awake. Taranis had explained that she had put most of the Opera into a deep sleep to allow the body to heal. The sleep helped aid an Opera's accelerated healing process. Aria's injuries hadn't been severe enough to merit a deep sleep, plus the reservations about a person with a concussion being put into a deep sleep.

Taranis took her eyes away from Jinto for a split second, "Get some rest, Opus 1, but try to stay awake. Stratton should be here soon."

Aria rolled her eyes; she hadn't even realized that she was sitting forward again. She resisted the urge to scoff about Stratton coming soon; the man seemed to be perpetually late. She didn't want to rest, though. She was too anxious about everything that had happened. She shuddered; she couldn't get the image of Light's motionless body out of her mind. She doubted that she would ever be able to un-see it. She knew that she shouldn't be focusing on her guilt right now. It would only further cloud her judgment.

"*Piano, have you found any more information on what happened?*"

"*Yes. I've been talking with the other AIs. Stratton was in a meeting with his higher-ups and wasn't able to give a command to contact you. Cadenza confirmed that it was an ambush; they took out her and Keiran first. Waltz told me about how Light managed to get the Opera to cooperate outside of teams.*"

Her stomach tightened again. She felt amusement crawl through her system, she imagined that Light had managed to get the Opera to cooperate through copious yelling and thinly veiled threats of violence.

"*If anyone could force them into behaving it would be him, or Keiran. They're both loud and not against threatening people,*" her voice was hollow. Aria was an Opus, Light's death had reaffirmed this. "*I feel awful about all of this...*"

"*I know. But Light wouldn't want you beating yourself up.*"

Aria pulled herself together just in time for Stratton to walk into the medical ward. She knew that he was ultimately there to talk with her, but she didn't want to deal with him yet. She watched him as he checked on each of his precious Opera, stopping to briefly chat with the ones who were awake. He said something to Jinto that made her friend laugh heartily. She then watched him make his way to the back of the ward, where Light's body was. She wondered if Stratton would inform Light's family about what had happened. After a moment of examining the body, he motioned for the nurses to take it out of the ward. He walked toward the bed Aria was on and motioned for her to follow him.

"Oh, no you don't. Major Stratton, Opus 1 leaving the ward was not part of our agreement. She has a severe concussion. You will speak to her here."

"No, I won't. You do not command me, Taranis. I need to speak to her privately," Stratton said calmly, it was one of the first times she had seen him exert chain of command on Dr. Taranis.

The normally fierce woman looked down at her feet, "Yes sir. You might need to help her walk. She's experiencing much disorientation upon standing."

Taranis helped Aria out of the bed. Upon being upright, the world turned upside down, which caused Aria to grab onto Taranis' arm. She wanted to be able to walk on her own, but she knew that she wouldn't be able to yet. Stratton came over and slipped his arm behind her back without a word. As they walked, the world started to right itself, but the floor felt like it was slanting a different direction with every step. He brought her to the closest private room to the medical ward, one of the interrogation rooms. He led her to one of the chairs and helped her sit down.

"What do you think he wants?"

"He probably wants to discuss the success of your mission," Piano said. *"He's very difficult to read right now. He's blocking me, but it's easy to see that he's very troubled right now. Be cautious."*

"Time to stop talking to Piano, Opus 1. Time to talk to me," Stratton said, pulling Aria away from her conversation with Piano. "I'm quite pleased that you brought Elegy back to us; she's incarcerated deep in the facility."

"I thought you were going to dispose of them."

"In due time. We need her alive," Stratton said, folding his hands into his lap. She had the distinct feeling that he was leaving something out. "If we kill her, we're afraid that the rest of Fugue will flee the area. With her alive, they'll stay in the area because 'they're not complete'."

Aria frowned; it didn't seem very ethical to keep Elegy alive for the sole reason of keeping the rest of Fugue in the area. But she knew it was smart and she knew that Stratton was right. If Elegy died, Fugue would no longer have a tie to Project Maestro. She wanted to hit herself over the head as well, she knew better than to think of ethics when it came to Project Maestro. If they had ever had an ethics committee, they never would have implanted AIs into children.

"Piano and I don't like the idea of killing them, sir."

"I know, but you do accept that killing them is one of our only options?"

Aria nodded. The two options she had managed to think of were killing them or imprisoning them for the rest of their lives.

Stratton seemed to be stalling and tiptoeing around the events of the previous day. Aria didn't like that he was stalling; it wasn't his style.

"With all due respect, sir, I don't see why you needed to pull me out of the medical ward. This is all information you could have said in front of the other Opera," she paused, her eyes meeting his and holding them. "Before we start, I have one question. Why didn't you pull me back? You gave me that stupid earbud for nothing."

"I simply wanted to express my pride in you. As for why I didn't call you back...there was nothing you could have done. The attack was quick and quite brutal. As soon as they started losing, Largo called for retreat," his voice was bitter. He sighed and put his head into his hands while he seemed to recollect his thoughts. "Fugue was created specifically for the purpose of destroying Opus."

Aria's jaw dropped. She had accepted that Opus had been deemed a failure and that a new specimen would need to be designed. Each of the Opera was exceptionally smart. They all had wanted to maintain their free will. They had all put Stratton through hell. She understood why the government would want a more compliant set of assassins. What she didn't understand was why this meant that the Opus project needed to be destroyed.

She looked up at him and said the only thing she could, "Why?"

"As I'm sure you've started to deduce, my idiot higher ups, especially General Crawford, decided that the Opus project had too much free will and that the results weren't high enough to keep producing Opera type assassins. They decided this despite evidence being in favor of Opera type assassins. There had been no major information leaks since the start of Opus," he stopped for a second, his face twisted in what appeared to be pain. "So I gave the government what they wanted. A six man team of assassins who have no free will. Their record on missions is abysmal."

"But why does that warrant thirteen...sorry, twelve...adolescents being killed?"

"Aria, I think he feels bad enough about this."

"I know. But I need to know why the government decided to have us killed off rather than something humane, you know, like letting us live."

Aria watched Stratton deflate back into his chair and scratch at his beard a little, "The government doesn't view their projects the way I view them. I view you as equals, as humans. They view you as mutants. And as you well know, anything different must be destroyed."

Aria did know this. She had read the stories about what had happened before and after the sky had been scorched. The changes the government had made had started before the sky had been scorched. Being homosexual had been outlawed. Adepts had been marked. There were still horrible stories going around about how the government was experimenting on homosexuals and the more unstable Adepts. Aria remembered that her parents had compared the government to Hitler. She had never thought of herself as a mutant. She had always thought that she was an 'enhanced human', which is what Stratton had told all the Opera to consider themselves.

"I've figured out that the lower intelligence is one of the differences between Fugue and Opus, as well as the hive mind. What else is different?"

"Fugue is a team. They only know how to be a team. An Opus knows how to work with others and by themselves. Fugue's field results have been so low because they could not work independently. I'm sure you noticed that Elegy was entirely different when she was off by herself," he stood up and paced behind the small table that was between them.

Aria nodded vacantly – her mind swimming. "Sir, I don't mean to contradict, but my field experience is against your existing data on Fugue," she paused as Stratton looked at her sharply, but motioned for her to continue. She started speaking again, slowly so she could keep the facts straight in her own muddled head. "They seemed to function better as a single unit, yes, but they are not useless on their own. You mentioned they were supposed to be flawlessly obedient – it's pretty clear that they are not. Is it possible that someone else could be controlling them? Your higher-ups maybe? Or that something just went wrong with their implantation?"

Stratton looked down at her, wonder mixed with an expression of self-hatred for not thinking of that planted on his face, "Both are entirely possible, though most of my higher-ups are too inept to do much of anything..." His voice trailed off for a moment. He cleared his throat and continued to divulge his knowledge. "Fugue naturally unnerves an Opus because of their lack of humanity. The only skills that Fugue excels in are tracking and stealth. If the element of surprise isn't on their side, they're useless. Opus 6 managed to turn the tide of their surprise attack and use our numbers..."

"Don't you *dare* talk about Light!" Aria said as she slammed her fists into the desk.

"Aria, no! Calm down!"

"No, I will **not** calm down. *Light was one of my best friends...*"

Aria and Light might not have always gotten along – but he had been one of her closest friends. He was one of the few people she trusted. And now he was gone and Stratton of all people was trying to talk about him.

Stratton looked taken aback for a split second, before his face shifted back into its usual schooled appearance. Adrenaline surged through her body, focusing the world that swam in front of her eyes. She lunged over the table towards Stratton. The man seemed to have regret etched all over his half-hidden face as he side stepped, grabbed her arm, and threw her to the ground without any effort. Aria popped up to her feet and reached for one of the chairs.

"No, no Aria. I'm stopping this..."

Piano crept into her limbs, not to help her, but to try and stop her. She fought tooth and nail against him and managed to get one hand clamped onto the chair. It was her body more than it was his, she would do whatever she wanted to do. She struggled against her seizing muscles to lift the chair. The second she got the chair high enough to be a threat, she felt arms wrap around her head and neck. Panic flooded through Aria's mind. It took her a second to figure out what had happened. Stratton had taken advantage of her internal struggle with Piano and sneaked up behind her.

Aria coughed and dropped the chair so she could grab onto Stratton's arm and stop the choke, "I yield. I'll stop."

He loosened the choke and Aria slumped against his arms, her hands wrapped around his forearms tightly. She didn't stop the tears that had been threatening to fall for hours. Stratton didn't berate her, he simply held her while she was shaking with sobs and grief.

CHAPTER 23

Aria was confined to her room for the time being, except for meals and some basic physical therapy. She had expected to be thrown into isolation after what she had pulled in Stratton's office, but he had quietly escorted her to her room and told her that Taranis would check in with her later. He had also mentioned that she wouldn't be going into the field until she was in a better emotional condition. She understood to an extent, but she was spending most of the day pacing around the small room. She wanted to make Fugue pay for what they had done to Light.

"I don't want to stay here," she said, her voice snappy and harsh.

"I know. But Stratton is right and you know it. You need to calm down before you pursue Fugue or you'll make bad choices. You won't be thinking clearly."

Aria knew that her AI was right. She wanted him to be wrong. She hadn't felt like this in ages, a combination of anger and bitter sulking. The last time she remembered acting like this was when she was around nine years old. Her parents had forbade her from performing in an important recital for various reasons. She understood now that performing for government officials went against everything her parents believed in, but at the time she had been furious. She had hidden in her room for days and had ignored her homework. Due to her poor academic performance that week, her parents had grounded her from recreational dancing as well.

A knock on her door pulled her away from her thoughts and she said, "I don't want to talk."

"You sure about that?" Jinto's soft voice said through the door.

She heard the door unlock from the outside and watched it swing open. Her friend limped into the room, leaning heavily on his black cane.

"You don't really have a choice in the matter, Aria. Stratton gave me the keys to your room," he said while spinning the keys in his free hand. She cursed internally – she had forgotten that all of the doors, despite being electric, had a key of sorts to open them when an Opus was being unreasonable. "I've wanted to check up on you for a while, but Taranis was keeping me in the medical ward until she was sure I was steady on this lovely cane."

Jinto shuffled over to the bed and sat down next to her. Aria sat stiff as a board, not knowing exactly how she was supposed to react to all of this. He was acting so normal, like nothing had happened. It just seemed wrong.

"Stop thinking like that, Ari. We all grieve in different ways," he said, his voice a touch sharper than it usually ways.

"S-sorry..."

Awkward silence fell between them, which put Aria further on edge. Normally she and Jinto could sit for hours without having to say something to each other. She knew exactly why the silence was awkward. Jinto wanted to talk to her about something that she wasn't quite ready to talk about.

"Alright, you need to stop pretending to be okay," Jinto said after about five minutes of silence. "We both know you're not okay."

She glanced over at her longtime friend, unnerved by the way he was able to read her. She let her head hang limply. Her AI buzzed comfortingly in her mind.

"I can read you so well because we've worked together for so long. It doesn't hurt that Andante and Piano are talking. You're my best friend. I've loved you for a long time, Ari. It *hurts* to see you like this."

She felt a pang in her chest. She and Jinto had been involved from the age of sixteen until the time she had left. It hadn't been anything too serious – they knew that they could die at any moment. She sat on her hands, not quite sure what she should do.

"I know...I'm sorry, Jinto," Aria said after another moment of silence. "I'm so angry and I don't know what to do with this anger. I want to make Fugue hurt for what they did to Light."

Jinto wrapped one of his arms around her shoulders before saying, "I understand that. Really. I would tear those bastards limb from limb right now. But more importantly, you need to turn that anger and grief into something productive. Right now you're just self-destructing. I heard you haven't been eating?"

"I haven't been hungry."

"That's a load of crap if I've ever heard one. Opera need food to function," Jinto said, whacking Aria on the back of her head. "Anyway, I'm going to help you work through your issues. Come on."

He stood up and walked towards the door; Aria followed him reluctantly. She just wanted to stay in her room. They walked through the habitation area, straight into the training room. She raised her eyebrow at him; Jinto had a serene smile planted on his face. He walked over to the wall and grabbed a kicking shield.

"I can't hit you, you're hurt!"

"I'm not as hurt as you think I am. Taranis already said I might need the cane for the rest of my life. I might as well learn to take hits again," he paused for a second as he shifted into a proper stance. "Bag sparring. Yell, scream, curse. Work out that aggression."

The bag sparring started slowly. Aria was still working through stiffness from her injuries and Jinto was getting back into the swing of fighting movement. Soon Aria was fighting with all her might, screaming curse words at Fugue. She pounded her fists into the bag until she felt the skin of her knuckles split open and start bleeding. She switched to kicks at that point, she didn't want to get too much blood on the bag. Her breath hitched as she shouted at the bag. Her chest constricted, she realized that she was crying. Aria fell to her knees, her hands pressed to her face as she continued to cry. She heard the kicking shield hit the ground with a soft thump. Jinto was kneeling next to her, his arms wrapped tightly around her body.

"I miss him so much..." she said, her voice strangled by sobs.

"I know, Ari. I do too. But he wouldn't want you to be unable to function," his voice was a little thicker than normal, Aria couldn't tell if it was from tears or the fact that his face was pressed into her hair. "Come on, let's get you to the medical ward so you can get those hands checked out."

Aria was to her feet first so she could help her friend to his feet. He might not be an invalid, but she knew how hard it was to stand up when injured. She pressed her hands against her camouflaged shirt, hoping she wouldn't leave a trail of blood.

"Opus 2, what did you do to her?" Taranis said, her voice hitting a pitch that Aria hadn't thought was humanly possible.

"She did it to herself. She's fine. We're just here as a precaution," he said, his voice slipping into what Aria referred to as his 'Opus' voice. It was the one he used when he was dealing with anyone but his teammates.

Taranis seemed to be pacified by this, but flocked toward Aria anyway. Aria instinctively resisted as the woman pulled her hands away from her shirt but eventually gave in.

"Well, you did a number on them. I thought no one was training yet?"

"That was my doing," Jinto said, flashing his most charming smile. "I promise I didn't do any of the hitting."

Taranis looked suspicious, but took what Jinto said at face value. She pulled Aria toward a curtained area to clean up her knuckles. The woman dabbed at them gently, revealing two large, bleeding burns.

"I suppose warning you that you'll need to take it easy will fall on deaf ears?"

Aria nodded.

"Well, I do have something that will speed up the healing process."

The substance felt like fire when it first touched Aria's skin. A moment later, it felt like her flesh was about to turn to ice. Once Taranis was convinced that there was enough of the salve slathered over Aria's knuckles, she motioned that she could leave.

"Um, would you mind if I plugged in? I haven't seen Piano in a very long time."

The woman smiled broadly and nodded while pointing at a computer in a corner of the ward. Aria made her way to the corner and pulled the long, black cord from the base of her neck. Soon she was greeted by the welcome rush of electricity washing over her body. Aria saw the white world of AIs come into focus. Her eyes snapped onto

Piano; she sprinted towards him and wrapped her arms tightly around his static-encased body. He stiffened in her grasp for a moment, but reciprocated the embrace just fiercely. The feel of his arms around her body relaxed her frayed nerves. She felt whole again. She hadn't realized it until that very moment, but it was like her mind had disconnected from real life.

"I miss them so much, Piano."

It seemed foolish to miss an AI, but Allegro had been part of Light just as Piano was a part of her. Also, she, Jinto, and Light had all plugged in together many times while they were on missions. She had gotten to know their AIs pretty well.

"I know. I do too. They were great friends."

Aria sat down on the ground and shivered as the digital signal engulfed her in white light for a moment, "I'm so sorry for how I was acting. I was being childish and you didn't deserve to deal with me. It was...it *is*...eating me up on the inside. I should have been able to do something for them. He shouldn't have been the one to die."

Piano sat down next to her, she thought his face looked strained, like he was trying to find the exact words to say, "I'd be more concerned if you weren't upset about this, Aria. It's natural to feel hurt and even guilt after losing a friend," he settled his arm around her shoulders. "I feel like we should have done something for them too. Allegro was a friend. But until this whole mess is done..." he paused for a second; his voice had a dark tone to it. Aria realized that he was still conflicted over what they had to do. "We should calm ourselves. Jinto was right. Grief is normal, but we need to be able to function."

"I know...we'll need to be strong for what's coming."

CHAPTER 24

Aria sighed to herself. She had learned that while Jinto's intentions had been pure, he had been genuinely concerned about her; Stratton had ordered him to help her work through everything. Once Stratton had realized that she had started her emotional recovery, he had started working with her on some basic training. A middle ground between the usual Opera training and the light physical therapy that Taranis had demanded she stick to for a while. It wasn't long after she started training with him again that she found herself on the roster for a mission. An off the books mission; she still felt conflicted for what Fugue had done to Light, but she was going to make them pay for it.

Aria found it hard to believe that she was already out on the hunt for Fugue again; the attack had barely been a week prior. She had tried to argue in favor of Jinto coming with her, but both Stratton and Taranis had stared her into submission. His injuries were still healing and possibly life-lasting; he was still adjusting to the possibility of having to use a can for the rest of his life. Then she had realized that it was probably because Stratton was acting of his own will – it would be easier to hide one Opus being gone, a squad would be much more difficult to make up a cover story for.

Some of the interrogation team, Stratton included, had tried to pry some information out of Elegy. Nothing had worked yet. She was finding that Stratton had been right. With Elegy still locked up in the Project Maestro facility, Fugue was staying relatively close. That gave her hope that her goal wasn't impossible. If they stayed close, she might be able to complete her task, even if it took her a long time. She knew it would be foolish to face them all at once.

"Are you getting any traces?" Aria said as she played with the buttons on the side of her goggles and looked around the surrounding area.

"Traces of all five AIs, but I can't tell if they're traveling together. They were here about ten hours ago. We're doing better than we did last time."

"Well, let's track the warmest of the trails, alright? Plot me a course toward that one."

Aria followed the directions that Piano gave her. The directions led her to an old, beaten up path that she wouldn't have recognized if not for her AI. She could see faint footsteps in the dust and couldn't help but smile. The old path had been a smart choice – but a road that didn't leave evidence would have been a smarter choice. The dust-covered path would lead her straight to them. Her stomach clenched, she couldn't help but think this was a trap. Fugue had to know that she would be the one coming after them and that Project Maestro would be vulnerable.

"*Honestly, I'm a bit nervous about that too. An Opus wouldn't do the same thing twice...it just seems illogical. But it is definitely plausible...*" Piano said, his voice calm, but cautious.

"*The plausibility frightens me. No one is really in fighting shape yet. It would be disastrous if they got to Project Maestro at this point.*"

They would be lucky if there was only one death if Fugue fought their way through Project Maestro again. When Aria had left, most of the Opera were awake, but weren't in fighting condition. She knew that Jinto and Madeline would fight. She knew they would get hurt or worse. She didn't want to deal with that level of grief all over again. She pushed the thoughts away and hit the buttons on the sides of her skates. A moment later she started powering towards where some or all of Fugue supposedly was hiding out. The terrain wasn't the best, but she would make do.

"*What's the nearest city that they might have gone to?*"

"*A moderately sized city called Quarterstaff. It's maintained by the government, but it looks like it's the only one in this general direction. It's also about ten hours on foot.*"

"*Sounds like we found we're going. Please set a course for Quarterstaff.*"

Aria smiled as Piano started giving her directions toward the city. The old path didn't provide her with much scenery, just dying tree after dying tree and grass so dead that it was gray rather than yellow. It was nice to be away from the facility; it was hard to be in the area that her best friend had been killed. It was hard to see a place that had been her home look broken. The loose dirt and dust on the path made it difficult for her to go as fast as she wanted to with her roller blades. She didn't want to risk sliding out and possibly injuring herself; she and Piano couldn't afford that at this point.

It took her and Piano about five hours to arrive in Quarterstaff. The trip had been uneventful, the area was so damaged that there were barely any animals nearby, much less humanoid threats. Quarterstaff was everything that Aria had expected of it. It was moderately sized, but quiet. It looked like it could get busy during the day. She was already starting to take note of the tactical hiding spots that she could use until they attempted to get whichever Fugue member they had followed. It wasn't an ideal city for anyone to hide in, but it would make due.

"Alright, let's see if they're hiding out in the city."

"Affirmative; scanning for any of the Fugue AIs."

Aria looked around again, this time activating the special feature on her goggles. She knew that it wouldn't be as effective in a more populated area, there would be more heat signatures in general and it would be harder to discern which ones were normal humans and which ones were possible Fugue members. She could only hope that Fugue was stupid enough to fragment and travel separately. It would be near impossible for her to bring in Fugue all at once; she knew she would have to bring them in one at a time. Even so, if they were traveling together, she would have to fight them all at once again. Somehow she doubted that this time would be any easier than the previous times.

She heard Piano start to say something but stop. He then said, "*Aria, they're not here...*"

"What? We missed them?"

"*It seems so. It looks like their signatures are moving towards Project Maestro again. I could be wrong, though. There's an outpost about five miles out that's open 24 hours for food. They might have gone there. But that seems like something you would do rather than what they would do.*"

"Something feels wrong about this, Piano. I don't like it."

She leaned back against one of the smog-strangled trees. Aria had known that Fugue would go back to Elegy, but she hadn't anticipated them acting so soon. In fact, it even made a bit of sense. The Opera at the facility were still injured, or at least just barely getting back into training. But she knew that none of them would be a huge challenge to fight. Fugue could take out almost all of Opus and retrieve Elegy to boot. It was a win/win situation for Fugue.

"*We'll wait here for a few hours. That will give them time to return if they're just at the outpost, but not too much time for them to get ahead of us if they're going back to Project Maestro. I have the roller blades.*"

I'll be able to catch up with them if we use the main road."

"That seems fair enough to me. Well-reasoned, Aria."

Aria made her way to one of the spots she had picked out, an area with some thick bushes. She slid underneath them and settled in on her stomach. The ground was cool and damp against the bare skin of her stomach, it almost made her relax. She adjusted the goggles over her eyes and tapped a button on the side. She zoomed in and examined the city with a cautious eye. There was excess residual heat in some of the buildings, but she had to dismiss it. She couldn't prove that Fugue had been in there, especially since they were nowhere to be seen. The heat vision was pretty useless unless Fugue was in line of sight. All humans left a residual heat signature, so did animals. Fugue just left 'more' heat behind than a normal human. But a faint Fugue signature might as well have been from a regular human. It was frustrating.

She turned onto her back and gazed up at the orange/gray sky through the skeleton branches of the bush. Aria had avoided stakeouts while she was away from Project Maestro. There were too many risks of doing them alone. She might fall asleep. If that happened, people could sneak up on her. She didn't have a second pair of eyes to help evaluate situations. Before she had ran away from Project Maestro; she, Jinto, and Light had excelled at missions that required stakeouts. She wished that she had been able to convince Stratton that Jinto be allowed to come with. Doing a stakeout by herself had her feeling off balance.

"I don't like the idea of doing this by myself."

"I don't either. But we'll make do. I'll take over if you get too tired," Piano said, his voice firm. "As much as I understand Stratton's reasoning about not letting Jinto come with, I really wish they were here."

Aria thought she heard a hint of fear in her AI's voice, but shrugged it away. She had heard it many times before. Whoever had designed the AIs for Project Maestro had given them exceptionally real personalities. Piano had never felt artificial to her, even when they had first bonded together.

She flipped back onto her stomach and buried her face her arms. It was going to be a long night. She couldn't chase away the feeling that something was wrong with the stakeout. Her gut was seldom wrong, but she hoped it was this time, for the sake of everyone back at the facility.

CHAPTER 25

Aria had been outside the city for about four hours when she was jolted from her thoughts by a sharp beeping noise. It took her a second to realize that it was the earbud that Stratton had given her. Her blood pressure spiked, a message couldn't be a good thing. She poked at the single button, which allowed the incoming message to be heard.

"Opus 1, pull back to the Project Maestro facility immediately. Fugue has returned. I repeat, return immediately, Fugue has returned."

"Damn it!" Aria said while jumping out of the brush and running towards the main road.

"*Piano, please plot a course from the main road. Fastest possible. We need to avoid checkpoints or anything that will slow us down too much.*"

"*Will do, Aria. But please, calm down. Your blood pressure is very high and your pulse is racing. Calm is what we need right now.*"

"Agreed."

Aria knew that her AI was right. She took a deep breath and fell back on her Opus training and consciously slowed her heartbeat. She had never been one to get too nervous about anything. Years of performing had beaten that out of her system at a very young age; but her friends and family being

202

in danger was like a panic button for her. She couldn't bear the thought of losing another friend.

She reached down and tapped the button on the side of her boots and felt the sides for the emergency feature that Stratton had installed on her skates for moments like this. While her skates were normally super powered and quite fast, there was now a turbo feature that allowed her to travel about two times faster than she was usually able to. She hit the switch and felt the turbo roar to life; then she pushed off. The new skates filled her with the most exhilarating adrenaline she had ever experienced. She was glad that she had her goggles on, otherwise her eyes would have almost instantly dried out.

Piano led her to the main road, finding the best ways to keep away from checkpoints. Aria had her Project Maestro issue ID in her pocket, but she didn't want to deal with the runaround that the guards would give. They would make her take off her boots so they could examine them, they would want to call in about her ID. It might even tip off Stratton's higher-ups and cause more problems. They didn't have the time to deal with that. Instead, Piano took them up along an old path once they got close to the one checkpoint they would pass.

Once they were safely on the path, Aria said as she bit her lip, *"How much longer are we looking at?"*

"Looks like about twenty minutes. At least that's what my calculations say. That turbo feature is amazing."

"*Well, your calculations are almost always right. And I really like this turbo feature; it almost makes me appreciate Stratton.*"

They emerged off of the path and the scenery started to get more familiar. Aria could see the bluffs; they were jagged against the horizon. She knew that the monolithic Project Maestro building was close. From the distance, there didn't appear to be anything wrong with it; but she knew that Stratton wouldn't have sent her a command if the facility was fine.

As Piano predicted, they arrived at the Project Maestro facility within twenty minutes. Aria was coated in a fine sheen of sweat and was breathing heavily. She turned off the turbo and made the wheels retract; after that, she sprinted towards the gates. She gave the guards a pointed stare before continuing her sprint toward the door that was clearly in lock-down mode. She wondered which of the 'secret' entrances Fugue had decided to use.

Aria started to pry the panel off the wall and said, "*What color to what color?*"

"Opus 1! NO! We need the building to stay in lock-down mode. Hard-wiring it might cause the rest of the building to exit lock-down mode. We can't risk that. Let me let you in."

Aria nodded stiffly and waited as patiently as she could for the door to open. She knew it was only a few minutes, but it felt like an eternity to her and she needed those moments. Once the door was open, she thanked the guard at Piano's urging, and started running towards the Opera wing. She felt an arm wrap around her waist and stop her from running.

"Let me go! Who the hell do you think you are?!" Aria said, her voice strained as she fought against the arms that seemed to be as strong as steel.

"Stratton. Now calm down. You can't rush into this fight."

"Aria, you know he's right. Stop fighting him."

Aria growled to herself but stopped fighting against Stratton. He set her down on the ground and Aria glared at him with all her might. She knew that both he and Piano were right, she couldn't rush into the fight and expect to win. There were five of them and one of her. Those weren't good odds, even for a fighter as skilled as she was. The only good point she had was that they wouldn't be able to surprise her. She slumped against the wall and allowed her body to fully relax.

"Are you okay?" Piano asked, buzzing around her mind.

"I'm...fine. I don't like the odds. The only time I fought all of them they were playing with me. I'm...I'm scared."

It made her feel sick to her stomach to admit something so simple.

"Opus 1, you seem to have calmed down quite a bit. We need to think this through a little more," Stratton said as he ushered Aria into a side room. "We have Fugue sealed in a room, for the moment. I figured there was a decent chance that they would attack once you went out to find them again, so I had the Opera who were ready to fight posted," he paused again, relief seeping through his usually schooled face. "The other Opera are safe for the time being."

Aria was pushed into a chair as Stratton found one for himself. She looked at his bushy beard and noticed how old he looked, even if he had been taking anti-aging pills. She had never thought of Stratton as an old man, but today he looked as though he was ancient.

"There were no casualties from this attack, thank god. But there were injuries. It's painfully clear that you're the only Opus well enough to fight Fugue. It's also clear that you're outnumbered and overpowered -"

"Sir, I've fought them before and won," Aria said, her voice cocky.

"You know as well as I do that they were only playing with you," Stratton said, his face creased in irritation. "Now they're fighting to get Elegy back to them. They will be far more brutal this time around. That...and I think you're right. Someone else is controlling them, or something went very, very wrong during implantation."

Aria narrowed her eyes; she could see Stratton's point even if it irked her. She knew that she was going to be more vicious now that she was protecting the people she cared about. She didn't know if she'd be able to survive such an intense attack. And the fact that he was admitting that he didn't know what exactly was wrong with Fugue made her scared as well. Stratton had always been the one with answers.

"I don't want him to know I'm scared."

"I know. I can sense fear on him as well. It's a bad situation for all of us."

When she spoke, her voice was even and calm, "I'll be careful."

She watched Stratton close his eyes tight, his chest heaving, as he swiped his left hand through his hair. Frustration was in all of his motions.

"Careful isn't enough. I'm almost positive that they're going to kill you...and...and I can't bear the thought of another Opus dying..."

Aria's chest tightened at the mention of Light and the hesitation in his words. It showed her that Stratton realized they were more than an Opus, which is why the government wanted them killed.

"It's touching that he realizes we're more than the program, but I think he's still concerned about saving face," Aria said to Piano.

"I wouldn't be so sure. Even if he was, I can't blame him. The government could make him disappear."

She let the indignation slide from her like sweat on a hot day; she knew that Stratton cared about all the Opera more than the government could ever know. It was foolish of the government to think that the man who looked after thirteen teenagers and adolescents wouldn't end up emotionally invested in his work.

"I'm aware that it's likely that I'll die. What you forget, sir, is that my friends and sister are the ones that Fugue wants to kill."

Stratton looked strained mixed with some other emotion that Aria couldn't identify. She assumed it was because he was beginning to regret recruiting the sibling of an Opus.

Aria's calm appearance betrayed her emotions. Her stomach felt as though thousands of bugs inhabited it, crawling around and biting everything. She imagined wrapping herself in ice to keep the fear that gnawed in her stomach under control, it barely worked. Yet she sat calmly and almost coldly before Stratton, her reserve unwavering.

"I just want you to make sure that you know the consequences of going to fight Fugue," Stratton lowered his intense blue eyes to his lap. She could feel tension radiating from him. "I...I need you to realize that you are going to die."

She took a deep breath with her eyes closed, just succeeding in keeping her fear at bay, "I am aware of my odds."

She stood up and started towards the door, but Stratton grabbed her arm. Aria looked back at him and then looked down at what he was holding in his hand.

"Opus 1, will you please take a gun?"

Aria looked at the gun; she had never been overly fond of guns. She knew it would even out the playing field. If she took the gun there was a slight chance that she might live and she didn't want to die yet.

She even understood why she had to go alone. Stratton was covering his tracks – trying to keep the government hounds off of his scent for just a little longer. Just long enough so he could save the others. Sending a firing squad, while quick and efficient, would mark him for death so fast.

She gripped her hand over the barrel and nodded as she said, "As a last resort." She tucked it into the back of her pants – finding a holster would waste time.

"That's the Aria that I know..." Piano said, his voice nearly inaudible, commending her reasoning.

"Good luck Opus 1, give them hell."

Stratton stood up and faced Aria and extended his hand as though she was his equal. Aria grasped it and nodded her head rigid as granite. She looked into his eyes and saw something she had never seen before; some sort of softness.

"Aria...I am so very proud of you. Be careful."

At that moment she knew that the order to destroy Fugue had come from his superiors. It really had been his own decision. It took all of her mental strength to turn away from him.

Aria let out her breath as she left the room. She was shocked to feel her legs shaking. She started down the hallway towards the Opera wing. There was only one containment room big enough for the five remaining members of Fugue. She knew it wouldn't hold them for long, because it hadn't managed to hold her for very long. When she was younger and before they had started sending them out on missions, Aria had become quite adept at escaping 'secured' rooms.

There was no blood on the walls to show Fugue's rampage. The facility almost looked normal, except for the flashing red lights that told her the building was in lock-down mode. The lack of evidence unnerved her.

"Piano, if it comes down to it, I want you to make me strong," Aria whispered as they reached the locked doors of the Opera sector.

"Are you sure? The stress is really hard on your body. It could cause more harm than good."

Aria smiled faintly, his concern always touched her. 'Making her strong' was code for him numbing her pain receptors so she didn't fatigue or feel the hits she took. It was dangerous. The one time she had used it sparring Stratton she had wound up breaking her ribs and not realizing it until she had punctured her lung. It had always been a last resort type move that she had utilized occasionally when she was out on her own.

"It's another fail safe. I don't want to rely on the gun."

It wasn't because she was unwilling to shoot them. It was that if Fugue knew she had a gun, they would do anything to get it away from her. Then her failsafe would be gone.

"I understand."

Aria pulled the panel off the wall, almost feeling guilty since they had just fixed it. She shook away the feeling knowing that guilt would just get in the way of her fighting. She matched the colors, for once remembering which colors went together. The door to the Opera sector slid open benignly, revealing nothing out of the ordinary. Aria made her way to the room where Fugue had to be contained and pressed her ear against the steel door. She couldn't hear anything, but she hadn't anticipated being able to hear through metal.

"Are they in this one? It seemed like the most logical choice..."

"They're definitely in there. They're trying to block me from sensing them; doesn't really work when there's five of them in the same room."

Aria's hand hovered over the keypad. She had no idea what the code was, but she knew that Piano would be able to get her into the room. Her stomach still felt like there were bugs crawling around in it, but she was far calmer than she had been when she was meeting with Stratton. Fugue was waiting for her. It was time.

CHAPTER 26

Piano guided Aria through the sequence to open the door. There was an electric whirring sound as the door started to slide open. She knew it would take a little longer, there were several series of locks and fail safes in the containment rooms. Aria felt her stomach knot up; years of performing disappeared from her mind, years of being Opus 1 vanished. She felt like a scared little girl and the fear made her feel human. There had been times she had been nervous, even frightened, during missions and when she was a mercenary on her own. Nothing she had experienced before compared to the level of terror that was pumping through her veins. It was almost refreshing.

The door seemed to take forever to slide open; once it did, Aria looked upon the members of Fugue with disdain. She recognized them all from the first fight, but Piano whispered their names anyway and reminded her of how they had fought during that first fight. She especially remembered Largo; the one who had hit the hardest. She wondered if he had been the one to kill Light; if he had, he would pay. Whoever had killed Light would pay.

She entered the room and immediately shot the internal panel, causing the door to slam shut and lock down. That would at least slow them down if they killed her. The door was too heavy to lift, but she knew they would eventually be able to get out. She took a deep breath and looked at the five Fugue members that were starting to surround her. Five on one was never good odds; but it would be worse if they managed to surround her. She knew that she would have to more vigilant than ever if she wanted to make it out of this situation alive.

"You're the one who captured Elegy," Diminuendo said, his voice holding an edge that hadn't been there the first time Aria had met him.

"Yes, I am." There was no sense in denying it. The Project Masetro databases would say that Opus 1 was the one who brought Elegy back to the facility.

"Give us Elegy. Fugue needs Elegy or it doesn't work right..." he said, the vulnerability returning to his voice, even though his eyes were murderous.

"I can't give Elegy back. Perhaps if you agree to come with me, Major Stratton will allow you to see her."

"I don't think reasoning with them is your best choice, Aria. I can feel their instability. They feel far more dangerous now than they did when you entered this room."

Aria knew they were more dangerous right now and it didn't take an Adept to feel it. She could feel the hatred radiating off of all five of them, it made the small hairs on the back of her neck rise towards the ceiling.

She had barely blinked when she sensed the attack coming. Aria brought her left arm up to defend from the blow that quick Grave had almost managed to pull off. While she had managed to block most of the hit, a shock of pain radiated through her arm. She slipped into a defensive stance, her hands up in front of her. One hand protected her face while the other protected her heart. It would be foolish for her to think that they weren't armed in some way, shape, or form. It was better to be cautious.

"Rondo from the right!" Piano said, forcing Aria's muscles to look in that direction.

Aria hardly had time to bring her right leg up to strike the girl in the stomach to halt her advance. She could barely keep up; while their attacks were coming one at a time, they were vicious. Sooner or later one of those hits was going to be too much for her and they would be able to overwhelm her. She needed to focus; her mind clearly wasn't in the fight yet.

Her moment of thought dropped Aria's attention just long enough for Largo, Rondo, and Diminuendo to swarm attack her into the solid steel alloy door. Her head slammed against it and her back arched in pain. She landed on one knee, her head bowed low as white spots danced in front of her vision. She saw a foot start plowing towards her. She grabbed it and pulled her attacker to the floor. She then pushed herself back

214

up, her blue green eyes leveling towards Largo. Her arms fell naturally into an aggressive defensive stance. She cursed internally as she realized that she was dancing around the task of destroying her enemies. Being defensive would get her killed. She needed to be on the offensive.

"*Piano, how much do my chances of survival go up if I go on the offensive?*" Aria said while parrying a punch from Stretto and chasing him away with a low roundhouse kick.

"*So much that if you don't go on the offensive yourself, I'm doing it for you. It is in your best interest to try and turn the battle in your favor.*"

Aria grinned to herself, despite her AI's threat. She closed her fists and finally looked around the room that she was in. It was larger than she remembered. She could use the size to her advantage, but they could use it against her just as easily. She wouldn't let Fugue get behind her, it they did, it was all over.

"*Alright, focus on scanning their movements and letting me know where they are. This should prevent them from getting behind me for a while. If that becomes a problem, I'll go into a corner...*" Aria whispered to Piano, hoping that he was dampening their conversation. With the other AIs around one couldn't be cautious enough. "*What do you think?*"

"*That should work well for now. I normally wouldn't agree about backing into a corner, but with the amount of enemies...I think it's a decent tactic...*" his voice trailed off for a second. "*I'll monitor your pain*

215

receptors as well. If you need me to, I will make you strong. Don't forget you have a gun."

Aria felt a chill go down her spine; she didn't like being reminded of her final plan to deal with Fugue. The gun was tucked into the back of her pants – she hadn't had time to find a holster. It was cold against her skin. She took another deep breath and looked at her five adversaries again. Even the ones she had hit didn't appear to be in pain. It only took a second for Aria to leap into action, her long leg sweeping into the shoulders of Grave, knocking her into Largo and Diminuendo. While they were down, she charged at Stretto and tackled him to the ground, bringing her elbow across the side of his face, knocking him unconscious. She felt an arm loop around her neck and she realized that she hadn't spotted Rondo. She grabbed onto the arm, twisted her body, and sent Rondo flying into a wall. She hoped they would stay down.

"Please tell me they're unconscious."

Piano didn't answer her. Aria knew that meant that he refused to tell her that they were already coming around. They must not feel pain the same way a normal human did – they had taken quite a lot of damage. Then again, so had Aria. Piano would let her know when she needed to know. Her brow furrowed as she nimbly dodged an attack that Largo was leading, silently thanking his massive telegraph. Diminuendo slipped through her guard and punched her across the right side of her jaw. Stars danced in front of her vision as she kicked him hard on the shin. She braced herself on the wall and wiped blood away from her face.

"What the hell are you doing? Think about what you're doing. Why would you want to kill Opus? Don't you realize that the government will dispose of you once you destroy Opus?"

"We were ordered to destroy Opus. That is our only order. Once that is done and we have retrieved Elegy, we are going to leave," Largo said calmly.

"Calm yourself, Aria. You can't reason with them."

Aria was about to reply to Piano when she felt a stab in her side. She tumbled to her knees once again. She saw Rondo kneeling next to her, a knife dripping blood in her hands. Aria knew that Rondo had meant to do damage, she had used a regular knife versus one with an energy blade. The energy blade would have cauterized the wound instantly. Painful, but lifesaving. Aria winced as she put her hand to the wound and looked at the candy coating of sticky blood.

"Scan if that hit anything vital, please."

"Didn't hit anything vital, but it's deep. You're going to need medical attention."

As Piano told her that, Aria kicked Rondo into the wall while grasping her side tightly. It hurt to breathe. Her breathing was ragged and the blue tank top she had been wearing was ripped badly and had a growing bloodstain. She almost wished that she had been wearing fatigues; they would have guarded her body a little more. She took a deep breath and ignored the blazing pain that it caused and pushed her physical pain to the back of her mind. She felt warmth spread through her limbs as her AI realized that her body was wearing out from the injuries. They both knew that the fight was going to be over soon and if she didn't change her tactics again, she was going to die. With her pain numbed, at least she would be able to fight without that clouding her judgment.

The anger that she had felt before melted away into fear and sadness as she reached for the gun that was pressed against her spine. She would rather be Stratton's pawn than be dead. She wanted to see her family. She wanted to see Babylon. She wasn't going to let Fugue stop her. She engaged Largo in combat, striking him on the ribs, hoping that he would drop to the ground. He merely looked at her in discomfort. While she was distracted with Largo, Aria felt cold hands wrap around her throat and lift her from the ground. She gasped and tried to shove him, her free hand's fingers wedging between the hands and her throat. She slammed the gun down over Diminuendo's head and fell to the floor, her face smashing into the cement floor. Aria could have sworn she felt something crack in her face and collarbone, but with Piano numbing her injuries it was hard to tell. Diminuendo crawled over her pinning her to the cement, his hands wrapping around her neck again. She wheezed for air and closed her eyes tightly.

"Not yet," she said, her voice gravelly. She raised the gun to his head and pulled the trigger.

The gunshot deafened her for a moment. Diminuendo slumped on her, his head created a puddle of blood and viscera on her shirt. She felt sick to her stomach as she pushed Diminuendo's body off of her and got to her feet. She hoped that Stratton was getting a force together. What she had just done was sure to make Fugue angrier than before. The rest of Fugue appeared to be too shocked to do anything for a moment. Grave, Rondo, and Stretto all charged at her at the same time. She felt Piano meld into her limbs and take aim with the gun. She didn't resist her AI's action, he would have better aim at this point in time. Before the three could even get to her, three loud gunshots rang out and their bodies hit the ground.

Aria brought her gaze to Largo, who had just sat by and watched as his teammates had been killed. She could see a small smirk playing on the corners of his mouth and she had the sinking suspicion that he had planned for them to be facing off in the end. She knew that wasn't in the nature of Fugue, but his expression said otherwise. Then again, she and Stratton had theorized that something was wrong with Fugue. Largo's entire posture and attitude seemed more relaxed now that his team was dead.

"I see that your AI is numbing the pain of your injuries so you can try and beat me," Largo said while walking towards Aria, his voice had lost the flatness that it had in previous meetings.

He grabbed the gun from her before she even realized that he was going to make a move for it. Aria tried to hide her shock, but knew that she was failing.

"You're trying to figure out how I knew? Don't worry, your secret is safe with me, I can just feel it in the air. No one else in this room could have sensed it."

Aria relaxed a little, but narrowed her eyes. It wasn't standard for an AI to be able to sense that. It didn't make sense for Project Maestro to make one of the AIs in a group of 'flawlessly' obedient assassins more advanced than the others. She had figured that Largo was the leader (unofficial and official, she guessed), but giving him an AI that was different didn't make sense. If it wasn't the AI then it was the host that was different.

"Good assumption. You're wondering why I'm so lucid in comparison to my former teammates. Stratton and Miss Marcellus made a mistake in selecting me for the Fugue project," Largo said silkily as he circled around her. "I'm an Adept. I'm very good at hiding what I am. But being what I am allowed me to retain my mind, everything that makes up what I am. I've been controlling the other AIs since we started training."

She threw up her mental defenses. Aria had never been amazing at keeping out Adepts; that had been one of Jinto's strengths. Any bit of protection would be good at this point. She didn't even know what his skills were.

"So that means when I beat you in our last fight, it's because your power was spread thinly between all six of you. Or you needed to let me win for some reason. Or you were just playing with me."

"A little of all three. It feels so wonderful to have all my power back in this body. Do you have any idea how frustrating it is to have five AIs trying to tell you what to do? The only reason I 'followed' that one order was to make them shut up. I left Elegy behind because she was the most annoying – did you know that they killed her?"

Aria shook her head. She hadn't known that. What she did know was that the more Largo talked, the more she believed that being a lucid member of Fugue had driven him crazy.

Largo snorted, "Like I'd believe an Opus. I can't believe that Project Maestro thought you would be a match for Adepts. You're *clearly* inferior, unfortunately, I will only able to control Fugue because of my AI," he laughed a little. "I won't be able to make you kill yourself – but that means that I get the pleasure of doing it myself."

She liked the situation less than she had when she entered the room. She let her eyes settle on his chest, that way she would be able to see if he moved. Aria knew that the situation was far more dangerous now; he had been moving slowly in their previous fights because he had been exerting energy to keep the other members in control. Her gun was gone and she was injured. It was hard to tell if she had done much damage to him. Aria

could feel herself shaking again, she couldn't
remember a time when she had felt so human, so
able to be defeated.

*"Do you think he's going to go on the offensive,
Piano?"*

*"He's hard to read, so I'm not sure. I knew there
was something different about him...he hides it well..."*
Piano's voice trailed off for a second. *"Be careful,
Aria."*

Piano's comforting buzz wrapped around her
mind, bringing her focus back to the fight. She
watched Largo for a moment. She could see him
shifting; he could attack at any moment. Aria
leaped into action, throwing as many attacks at
Largo as she could. Her eyes widened in horror, he
was faster than she could have imagined. She
hated fighting his type; fast and strong. He was
countering every single attack with brutal ease.
She dropped to the ground as his instep connected
with her stab-wound. Aria coughed violently and
watched as blood spattered on the ground in front
of her. Even with Piano eliminating her pain, she
could feel the pulsing in the wound. She wiped
the blood away from her mouth.

"Good, stay down," Largo said, his ice blue
eyes thin as a snake's. "You won't be able to beat
me."

"Aria...get up!"

"I have an idea. Trust me."

Aria knew that Largo was right. He was too
fast, too strong, and able to read her movements.
He stood above her, leering at her. She hooked his

ankle with her heel and used her other leg to kick straight at his knee. He slammed into the ground with a scream. A second later she was standing up. She glared down at Largo and brought her foot down across his face. Aria heard him cry out as his nose broke. She felt bad for a split second; her kick had probably broken his knee. Breaking his face had been overkill. She turned and started to walk away.

"You lose, Opus 1," Largo said, his voice distorted by blood.

Aria turned around to face him, he was still on the ground, but he was pointing a gun at her chest. Her gun. The one that had been across the room. Her eyes widened as the sound of the shot rang through her head and hit her directly in the heart. Her body fell to the ground.

CHAPTER 27

It was a mere two days after Aria had been told that she was being implanted with a bio AI. Major Stratton was rushing her down the hallway towards the implantation room. She was nervous and excited, all of the students were. A bio AI would help her learn complex theories in no time. She needed all the help she could get; she was the very youngest in the group of very bright teenagers that Project Maestro had recruited.

They walked through the complicated series of hallways until they reached the implantation room. Aria was certain that she'd never be able to remember them. Stratton handed her off to the team. She could see that General Crawford, one of Major Stratton's higher-ups, was here as well. His smile seemed a little sinister in her mind.

"Hello Miss Brayton," one of the implantation team said; the voice distinctly male. "My name is Elijah Freeman and I'll be assisting Dr. Marianna Taranis with your implantation. If you would please lie down on this table, face down, that would be greatly appreciated."

Before she complied, she saw the telltale Adept tattoo on the left side of his head. Eli sat next to her and explained everything that he was doing.

He pulled her hair up off of her neck to keep it away from the incision they would make. He gave her an IV to make sure she stayed hydrated during the procedure. When she fought against the restraints that held her down against the table, he explained that it was for her own safety. They didn't know how the host would react when the AI was implanted. He also explained that putting her under wasn't an option – they wanted the host awake and alert. Aria jerked as coldness pressed against the back of her neck.

"It's alright, girlie. It's a sanitizing agent. Dr. Taranis is going to make the incision now," he slipped his hand around hers. "Just try to stay calm."

Aria grimaced as felt burning pain run in a line against her spine. She heard Dr. Taranis ask for the bio disc and felt pressure in the incision. And then nothing happened.

"Would you please grab me some glucose, dear?" Dr. Taranis said to one of the team members. Her voice was calm, but Aria sensed that this was a front.

Eli's hand was still wrapped around hers, but more tightly than it had been before. She felt the glucose push through the intravenous needle into her arm. It was cold and it made her dizzy, even though she was laying down. Her vision blurred to the point that the people around her just looked blotches of color and none of them could hold her attention for more than a second. Her eyes drooped shut as the room started to fade to black.

Everything hurt as Aria opened her eyes. She realized that she was in the medical ward, but had no idea how she had arrived there. She tried to remember, but her memory was blurry and it felt like her head was stuffed with cotton. Despite that, she could feel a second presence in her mind. It wasn't intrusive in the slightest, it almost seemed like it was waiting for her to become aware of it. She knew that it had to be the bio AI, but she was surprised that it hadn't introduced itself yet.

"I was waiting for you to be a little more conscious. My name is Piano," the AI said to her. The voice was gentle and calm, Aria had trouble defining which gender it was. After a moment of thought, she determined that it was male.

Aria jumped, while the voice was quiet and comforting, it was a new sensation and just felt weird. She didn't know how she was supposed to respond to him. Major Stratton hadn't been able to give an answer and neither had any of their teachers. They said it would be best if the students figured out how to communicate on their own. She wondered if she would always be talking to herself.

"How do I talk to you?" Aria said, her brow furrowed deeply under her dirty blonde hair.

"It's just like talking, but in your mind. Just carry out the conversation within your mind."

She scowled for a second, it couldn't be that easy. It had to be more complicated to speak with her AI. She shook away that thought, she needed to stop being so contrary.

"*Like this, Piano? My name is Aria, but they call me Opus 1.*"

She felt a comforting buzz in her mind and she instantly relaxed. Aria hadn't realized that every muscle in her body had been tensed, she had been far more nervous than she had thought. She wasn't a nervous person; her dancing had taken care of that. She saw the doctor approaching her, they had realized she was awake. Upon closer inspection, Aria saw that the woman was pale and shaking, almost like she was on edge.

Aria started to sit up as the doctor approached, but felt her muscles burn and whine. She was glad that implantation could only occur once. If this was how she felt afterwards she was pretty sure she never wanted to go through that again. The woman pushed Aria back against the bed with a scowl that clearly said 'you will stay put until I say you can move." Aria remembered Eli Freeman introducing the doctor, but couldn't remember her name. The woman was checking her vitals feverishly, her nimble hands flying from wrist to neck and then checking the IV that Aria had failed to notice was still there.

"*Her name is Dr. Marianna Taranis. She is in charge of implantation as well as making sure the health of the Opera is in superior condition. She will also be teaching the advanced science courses.*"

"*Thank you, Piano.*" she smiled as she communicated with her AI.

"Dr. Taranis, why am I in the medical ward?" Aria said, her mouth bending down into a frown.

"Post-implantation standard operating procedure. We need to monitor vitals afterwards and make sure everything went well."

Aria nodded, that made sense. She knew that messing with the human brain was dangerous. It made perfect sense for the host to be monitored after the implantation process. She cringed at the sudden pain in her arm; Taranis was pulling the IV out as gently as possible.

"Good job, Opus 1. If you'll follow me, please."

"*Why does my body hurt so much?*" Aria asked Piano as she worked at sitting up.

"*The implantation process is hard on the human body.*"

Aria had a feeling that Piano was omitting information from the story, but she didn't feel like pressing the issue. It was more important to make a strong connection with her AI so they would be able to work together flawlessly. She tried to push herself off the bed, but again, her muscles cramped and tightened. She closed her eyes and pushed off the bed again, this time it felt like Piano stretched into her limbs and helped ease her burden.

"*Thank you.*"

"*Not a problem. If you need help, I will always be there.*"

Aria followed Taranis in curiosity. The woman led her to a computer and had Aria sit down in the chair in front of it. Again, Taranis took her vitals, seemed satisfied, and then knelt down next to her.

"We're going to plug you into the computer."

"...What?"

"This is going to feel strange. Your AI will explain everything."

Taranis reached to the back of Aria's head, along the painful stretch of skin that had been incised to implant the bio disc. From the incision, the nurse pulled a long, thin cable and plugged it into the computer. Aria was hit with a wall of energy, buzzing around her. Unlike when Piano had buzzed, this felt like it was trying rip her apart. The energy was twining around her limbs and it felt like it was trying to suffocate her. She tried to scream, but no noise left her mouth. She fought against the rush of energy, but it wrapped around her and brought her to a quiet, peaceful place. When she opened her eyes she was in a white world that seemed to glow and hum with energy, the same energy that had pulled her in. Aria stood slowly, the pain in her muscles was gone but she felt disoriented and dazed. She took in her surroundings, while everything appeared bleached, she could see silver lines on the ground beneath her feet. There were hints of other colors every once and awhile. They were so faint, almost too faint to determine what color they actually were.

"I see you made it safely," a starting-to-be familiar voice said.

"...Where am I?"

Aria looked directly and what had to be Piano. He was very dark in comparison to everything in the surrounding area. His hair was dark brown, nearly black and very neat. Yet it still managed to fall into his eyes. His eyes were a pale green, like the color of good celery. He stood a few inches taller than her, or at least it appeared that way.

"This is the digital realm of AIs."

She looked at Piano in disbelief. She didn't understand how she could be in a different realm. Aria understood that it was entirely feasible, but she had just been plugged into a computer. She sat down on the humming floor, which instantly calmed her. The hum felt the same as when Piano had buzzed in her mind. While she felt entirely out of place, the clean white world was comforting. She saw Piano smile as she didn't argue the fact that the realm could exist. She figured it was because he wouldn't have to try and explain it even more. He lay down next to her on the white ground.

"So, Aria, what were you before you came here?" he asked, what appeared to be genuine interest laced through his voice.

She knew that he could just look up her file in the Project Maestro database, but appreciated that he would rather learn for himself.

"You called me Aria," she said, her eyes wide. "No one has called me that since I arrived here. They've either called me Opus 1 or Miss Brayton..."

"You introduced yourself as Aria. That means it is the name you identify with. I couldn't call you by a name that you don't identify with."

Aria smiled, hearing her real name was always nice. She had only been at the facility for a few weeks. They had been given codenames within hours of arriving. She had thought it was amusing and could be a fun game, but her friend Jinto thought it was more nefarious than that. She had no idea why she had been given the codename of Opus 1, other than for the arbitrary reason of her being the first one implanted with an AI.

"I was a dancer. Before Project Maestro recruited me I was to go to New York for a dance school. Though...Major Stratton has been kind enough to let me continue my dance practices on my own," she put her hands behind her head, her hair curling around her fingers. If she closed her eyes, it almost felt like she was at home again. "What's the different between a bio AI and a standard AI unit? They kind of explained it to us in one of our classes, but they weren't thorough enough for any of us to really grasp the concept."

Piano sat up, his face contorted in thought, "A bio AI is one that latches itself into the human nervous system. It's essentially two separate consciousness in one mind. A standard AI unit doesn't latch onto the nervous system and therefore will not take in the human mind. If you were using an exo-skeleton suit, though..."

His explanation was moderately better than the one that Miss Marcellus had given them, so she nodded in understanding. She looked over at Piano once more. He seemed very human for an artificial intelligence. His emotions didn't seem robotic, Aria thought whoever had programmed him had done an excellent job. He seemed just as real as any person she had ever met.

CHAPTER 28

Aria opened her eyes, her whole body ached. She had been shot through the heart; she knew that she couldn't have survived that. She sat up slowly and looked around; she was definitely not in the containment room. She was surrounded by long white grass that had silver lines running through them. She looked up at the sky; it was an indescribable oceanic blue, most closely called aquamarine. The sun was a vivid orange. The unscarred sky sent shivers down her spine.

Her mind felt strange, empty and alone. Aria reached out to Piano within her mind, but no comforting voice or buzz responded. She didn't understand how he could be gone. It was fatal for him to be removed. If he was gone, she was dead. Yet she was conscious. Aria pushed herself to her feet, the grass tickled her calves and her hair brushed her lower back. She didn't know how her hair was long again, but she didn't question it. She took a quick look and saw that it was her favored bright pink as well. She drank in her surroundings; there were only wide expanses of waving, white grass and the stark contrast of the white of the grass and the beautiful blue sky on the horizon. She felt bitterly alone.

"Glad to see that you're finally awake," a warm, familiar voice said.

"Piano? Where *are* we?"

She looked at him; he looked exactly as she remembered. Dark brown hair, light green eyes, and a few inches taller than her. The only thing that looked different was his clothing. She had never really been able to make out his clothing before because of the electrical static. He was wearing practical clothing in dark greens and browns. While he looked exactly as he always had, something just felt off.

"We are in the realm of AIs," he said, motioning for her to follow him. "Let's find a better place to talk."

Piano held his hand out for her to take, which she did without hesitation. Her fingers twined with his. She had relied on him for ten years, she wouldn't stop that trust just because they were in a bizarre place. He led the two of them to the edge of an amazing cauldron. On the far rim of the cauldron was a monolithic city. There were vehicles buzzing through the air of the city and some going far past it. Everything was so beautiful. Piano motioned for her to sit down near the edge of the caldera, she complied while staring at the flying vehicles.

"I assume you have many questions."

"Yes, I do."

There were questions begging to be asked, yet no words came to her mouth. After a moment of silence, she said, "How is this the world of AIs?"

She watched Piano smile a little to himself, it looked like he was debating on how to answer.

"You do have a way of picking the hardest questions," Piano muttered to himself. "Remember when you asked me about bio AIs?"

Aria smirked, she did remember, it was when she had first met her AI face to face, "Yes, but that hardly seems relevant."

"It's entirely relevant. The bio AI is the secret to everything."

A palpable silence hung between them. Aria had known that the bio AI was different and that the different made them important, but none of the Opera had really grasped the subject. No one had explained it well enough for her to understand and she hadn't been able to find any information on them.

Piano's face looked pained before he said, "The death of a human is an interesting thing. The body dies as expected, but the human consciousness is so much more than decaying organic matter. It breaks down into electrical signals and data. As you know, data cannot be destroyed."

Aria was holding her breath, what Piano was saying was hard to digest, but she trusted what he was saying. She knew that he was right.

"So instead of being destroyed, the data gets...transferred...to another universe, like this one. The data reincarnates as your personal image," he paused for a second and took some of Aria's hair into her hand. "This is why your hair is long and your favorite shade of pink."

"But how does this make this the world of AIs?" Aria interrupted her voice strained and impatient. She just wanted to understand.

"I'm getting there," Piano said patiently, his eyes closed for a moment. "There's a lot to explain. The dimension we're in is one above Earth. Instead of three dimensions, we have four. It'll take a little to get used to once you start using it. However, we can reach to Earth and when we do that, Adepts are able to become aware of our presence. Most people would say we're ghosts, they just can't understand us because this universe has more dimensions."

Aria nodded a little, she was following him well but couldn't see how this was leading to a relevant answer.

"One of the people who became aware of us was a member of a government run program that eventually became Project Maestro. They discovered that we could be trapped and used to enhance the abilities of humans," he paused again, his mouth partially open; his hands were fidgeting in his lap. "I'm still fuzzy on how it works...it's very confusing, especially when you're involved in the process. What I've gathered is one of us would reach through to Earth, since we're essentially data, we could be caught and 'stored'. I was caught, obviously."

Aria played with the long white grass while saying, "So...a bio AI is a human that has died, but whose consciousness lives on and is then captured?" a small nod said she was correct.

"When you would plug in, I would partially transmit back to this world and would partially bring you to it as well. The whole place was blurred with electrical static, which is why you could never see the colors or what I was wearing. Also, you were only a three-dimensional being at that point."

The only thing that Aria seemed to be able to do was nod. The whole thing seemed farfetched, but it seemed right as well. It made more sense than anything she had heard about afterlife. And she was no stranger to other dimensions. Night City had been on another horizon.

Aria brought her eyes to Piano and said, "Who were you before you died?"

Piano fell silent and Aria watched his face go through several different expressions ranging from sorrow to frustration. It was clear to her that his past was a painful topic. She almost regretted asking the question.

"I died in...2005. My name was Brad. I prefer the name Piano now. I was barely eighteen years old when I died – horrific car accident. I can't remember any of it now. For a while I thought I could...but I can't anymore. I don't want to remember. I was a piano virtuoso from a very young age. They thought it would be funny to give me the codename of Piano. I was on my way

237

to college to study music so I could have the degree that said I was as good as I was. I'm not Brad anymore though..."

Aria leaned back into the soft grass; this world was not marred by war. She couldn't comprehend belonging here. Even when she had been in Night City, it was clear that there were struggles between ideals. Her thoughts drifted to Project Maestro and her stomach tightened. She wondered what the outcome had been. She closed her eyes and inadvertently felt herself pulled towards what had to be Earth. She found herself standing in the containment room. She saw Largo on the ground, captured. Stratton was standing above him; his face was contorted as he leveled a gun at his prisoner. He pulled the trigger. She watched Stratton collapse to his knees in tears, punching the ground while sobbing that he was sorry. Sorry for everything he had done. She heard him choke out the words "I'm so sorry, Aria. I'm so sorry my beautiful baby girl."

"Aria, come back."

Aria's mind snapped back to the strange colored world that was now her home. She could feel moisture on her cheeks, she couldn't remember crying. Stratton had called her his baby girl.

"What happened? How did I get there?" she asked, her voice shaking so badly that it sounded like she was stuttering.

"You will find that it's incredibly easy for us to phase back into that universe. The slightest thought toward that world can pull towards it. It takes time to get used to it. You need to be careful, they can sense us. It's a good thing Stratton was a bit distracted, he's a powerful Adept."

She shivered; her body was covered in a fine sheen of sweat. Aria looked at her knees while she said, "I...I didn't know he was an Adept. What else do you know about him?" There was a challenge in her voice.

Piano looked at her with regret in his eyes, "A few choice pieces of information that I was told to never tell you under any circumstances. One was his status as an Adept. He's hidden it from the government for longer than you've been alive..." his voice trailed off for a second, hesitation was in all of his motions. "He was involved in a plot to stop the government from scorching the skies as well. The final is who your birth parents are. Stratton is your father, Aria. Your birth mother is Miss Marcellus."

Aria didn't know how to react. She didn't understand how she hadn't seen it for all those years she was at Project Maestro. Now it was obvious. They had eyes that were the same size and shape. She had a feminine version of his jawline. She felt Piano place his hand over hers. The small action of comfort and companionship calmed Aria's rough nerves.

She knew deep down that the government was going to try and eliminate Stratton within the next few hours to the next few days. General Crawford was sure to find out who had ordered that Fugue be killed. She hoped that he and her fellow Opera would be able to escape the government's wrath. She looked up at Piano, she could tell that he knew the thoughts that were going through her mind. They had been together for ten years; they were able to read each other too well.

"Project Maestro will be done. Another government run program will take its place, though. There will always be another."

She knew the words were true, but she let them slip from her mind. Aria didn't want to think about the government anymore. There were questions trying to slip out from her lips, but she bit them back. There would be other days for questions, other days for deep discussions. She wanted to know everything about this new world and she knew that Piano would teach her in time. He had always taught her and she knew that he wasn't going to stop now.

"If you aren't Brad anymore, who has Piano become?" Aria asked, her voice as soft as the grass that surrounded them.

"I've become a teacher. Quiet and calculating, a bit of a hacker even. Part of me thinks I've forgotten how to play the piano."

"You'll never forget something like that. It stays with you forever," she said, her hand warm in his. "Are Light and Allegro here too?"

"Yes, don't let Light fool you. He's happy that his best friend is here, but he'll yell and scream at you because you shouldn't have come so soon."

That's how Light had always been. He would snarl at her because he cared about her.

"That means Largo is here too..." she said, her voice barely a whisper. "And the rest of Fugue."

"Don't let the picturesque world fool you, Aria. This place has seen war. Should Fugue become a problem – they will be dealt with."

They stood up and started making their way to the city cell in front of them. The silence between them was companionable, as it had always been. Aria looked at the man she had been with for ten years and smile. He returned the smile; his smile slow and unsure in comparison to her broad grin. They didn't need to say the words to know what the other was thinking. They wrapped their arms tightly around each other, their faces inches apart. The questions tried to escape Aria's mouth again, so she buried them deep in the back of her mind. She brought her face close to hiss and kissed him deeply.

"One last question for today..." Aria said softly, Piano nodded. "Dance with me?"

She ran towards the city, Piano following close behind her, both laughing like they had never seen horrors. Her hair streamed behind her, the orange sun making it look like pink fire. She was with the man she had loved for years; she didn't need to worry about being Opus 1 ever again. She knew that her father would take care of the other Opera. She would worry about the tribulations of this new world another day. For now, she wanted to dance. She was free to just be Aria.

EPILOGUE

John Stratton sat at his desk, swirling whiskey in a glass. His daughter was dead. Aria was dead and she had never found out that she had been his daughter. The only real consolation was that he had been the one to pull the trigger on Largo, the psychotic leader of Fugue who had killed her. He knew that General Crawford was bearing down on the Project Maestro facility. He had already evacuated most of the guards. He had issued an order to Marianna Taranis – she was to gather the remaining Opera for a meeting. He wanted to get them as far away from the facility as possible. It was going to turn into a warzone. Of course, he had a plan for that too.

He jumped a little as he heard the doorknob creak a little – he decided now was the best time to down his shot of whiskey. John relished the burning sensation. Today had been one of those days where you just needed a drink.

He had been having those days a lot lately. Between Fugue, one of the Opera dying, and now his daughter dying, he had gone through a lot of whiskey.

"John...is it true?"

He looked up and saw his wife Darien Marcellus, her face pale and lips quivering a little. He didn't want to say it. He had to say it though. He couldn't lie to Darien.

"Yes. Aria was killed this afternoon. It was...it was my fault."

John looked up from his lap, Darien wasn't crying, she was just sitting in shock. Her hands were resting on the armrests of her wheelchair, like she was poised to stand up. He could feel her emotions swarming through the room, joining his own.

"Did you kill the person who did it?" she asked her voice cold as ice. He recognized the feeling of her burying her emotions.

John nodded, unable to form a sentence. It always threw him a little off balance when Darien buried her emotions like that. It made her feel unnatural, inhuman.

"Good. I assume Crawford is on his way here with an 'army'?"

He relaxed a little, "Yes. He is. I've evacuated most of the staff. It's just the two of us, Marianna and Eli, and the rest of the Opera left on base."

Darien nodded a little. She pressed her hands against the armrests and pushed herself to a standing position. She beckoned John over – he couldn't deny her when she was actually standing. That didn't happen very often. He wrapped his arms around her tightly and buried his face into her white blonde hair.

"You know I voted against both Aria and Maddie?" Darien said, her voice sounded a little strangled.

"Yes. I know, Dari. Crawford forced us to take them on due to their scores and the fact that they look so much like us. I might hate the man, but he isn't *that* stupid. I'm surprised the girls didn't catch on."

Darien snorted, "They hate you. They wouldn't want to associate their looks with you."

"You're right," he sighed. It felt weird to act so normal. "I trust you've been prepping for our plan?"

Another laugh from his beautiful wife, she collected herself and said, "Of course. Those sons of bitches won't know what hit them."

John rested his head on top of hers, a smile that almost seemed unhinged spread over his face. Their plan was foolhardy. He knew that. But between him, Darien, Eli, and Marianna; they had enough firepower to stop an army. Crawford was going to regret the fact that he forced them into working for the government. He was going to make damn sure he regretted everything.

About the Author

LL Lemke is a writer and martial artist from Oconomowoc, Wisconsin. She has been a huge fan of science fiction and fantasy since she was little and she still wants to be a superhero. She has always had a soft spot for villains in fiction. She holds a BA in Creative Writing from Carroll University. Opus Aria is her first novel.